UNEXPECTED

UNEXPECTED

B. RAE GREEN

iUniverse®

UNEXPECTED

iUniverse books may be ordered through booksellers or by contacting:

iUniverse
1663 Liberty Drive
Bloomington, IN 47403
www.iuniverse.com
1-800-Authors (1-800-288-4677)

ISBN: 978-1-4917-9072-4 (sc)
ISBN: 978-1-4917-9073-1 (e)

Library of Congress Control Number: 2016903024

Print information available on the last page.

iUniverse rev. date: 03/10/2016

Dedicated to my daughter Tracy, my son-in-law Chuck

and my handsome grandsons

Garrett and Jacob

and my babies

Punkin' Rae, Mo and Misty

And to my very dear friend Nancy

Without her this book

would never have been written

CHAPTER 1

WHEN JEFFREY PRESTON Harriman got up that morning, he felt like the day was going to be different, somehow. He couldn't put his finger on it because everything seemed to be in order. He woke at the same time, took a shower and dressed like he always did. He left the house at 5:00 a.m. as usual and found Albert waiting to take him to the studio. He used Albert as his driver, not because he was showing that he had the money for that, but because he liked to study his scripts in the quiet of the car.

Home was a fifteen-acre estate in Beverly Hills. He became the owner of the property by way of his grandfather. They had adored each other and Jeff missed him greatly since his death. His parents, Joe and Mary, still lived in the house with him. He liked having them here with him. Not only had his father lived there all his life and his mother since her marriage to Joe, but because he loved and respected them. Nobody got in each other's way, but were still there if they needed each other.

The studio was where he practically lived. He was in a television series that filmed in Culver City and he spent long hours there during the week. He suited his part well and seemed to have a natural talent. He was modest about that talent by saying that since he was independently wealthy, he was more relaxed in his acting. His fellow actors disagreed, noting that Jeff worked harder than any of them to make the show as good as possible. The viewers must have agreed because his show was almost always in the first or second spot for top ratings.

Walking into the studio on this day, Jeff looked around and noticed several new people on the set. One of them came over to him and asked if he would like a cup of coffee. After telling her how he liked it, she took off to get it for him. Watching her as she went to get it, he realized he was getting that feeling again that he had had that morning.

"Mr. Harriman, Mr. Harriman. I have your coffee here, Sir," she said gently, waking him from his reverie.

"Jeff, please. No one calls me Mr. Harriman or Sir, for that matter," he told her. "What's your name?"

"Leslie Garrett," she said.

"Well, Leslie Garrett, what's your job here?"

"I do extra work when they need me, and I also run errands and do whatever needs done."

"I hope you have a great experience here with us, Leslie."

"Thank you, Mr. er Jeff."

As she took off to get set for the next shot, Jeff saw Skip and went over to him. "Skip," he said. "What's the story on the new girl, Leslie Garrett?"

"Boss, she came here from Ohio, she's a widow with a four-year-old daughter. She lives in East L.A."

"How do you always know so much about people?"

"I don't know," he shrugged. "I guess they just love to tell me things."

As Skip wandered off, Jeff knew that this meeting with Leslie was what gave him the feeling he had this morning.

CHAPTER 2

A S THE SEASON went on, Jeff saw very little of Leslie. She brought him his first cup of coffee in the morning, but then she was busy doing work as an extra or running errands for those who needed her. But, he never lost that feeling he had the first day he met her.

One morning when she brought him his coffee, he noticed that she wasn't acting as cheery as normal. He asked her what was going on.

"I'm getting a cold," she said, blowing her red nose. "It's nothing, really. I'll be better soon."

Taking in her appearance, he asked, "I realize it's not polite to inquire about a lady's weight, but have you been losing some lately?"

"You know what they say about the camera and ten pounds." She seemed to be in quite a hurry to get off the weight subject. "I've really got to go now, Jeff. They need me in this next scene."

"Wait a minute, Leslie. I want you to take my card. If you ever need anything, please feel free to call me. Promise?"

Hesitating, she seemed unsure about his motives. Noting her hesitation, he quickly assured her that he had no ulterior motive.

Taking the card and putting it in her pocket, she promised.

CHAPTER 3

FINALLY, IT WAS Friday. When Leslie got home that night and had picked Emma up from Mrs. Wright, the babysitter who lived downstairs, she had never regretted her fourth-floor walkup more. Her cold was getting worse and she felt like she had a fever.

"Mommy, why are you so slow today?" asked her four-year-old. "I've been upstairs and back down again."

"Honey, Mommy doesn't feel very good tonight."

"'Cause of your cold?"

"Yes. It'll be ok. Let's get you upstairs so you can eat your supper. Nancy made you a special one today. I think there's a piece of chocolate cake in here."

"Oh, I love chocolate cake." Hurrying ahead, she waited for her mother by the door to apartment 4D.

Finally making it to the door, Leslie let them in and got Emma settled at the kitchen table. She opened the food containers that Nancy had fixed for her and made a plate for her daughter, as she did every night. Money was tight and they were lucky that Nancy fixed these food boxes for Emma every night they were on set.

Apartment 4D was a fourth-floor walkup in East L. A. It wasn't the best neighborhood, but it was the best she could do for her budget. Mrs. Wright was a wonderful babysitter for Emma. Leslie knew that Emma was safe there, and that was the most important thing to her.

The apartment was what you would call "lived in." Leslie had tried to personalize it by adding the few things she had brought from Ohio. She had a few pictures of herself, her husband Troy, and Emma. She also had her grandmother's quilt. Other than clothes and a few toys of

Emma, these were all that she had. She had no family and had felt so alone since her husband died when Emma was a year old.

Of course, being small you didn't really need a lot of stuff to fill it. There was a tiny kitchen with a table that took up most of the floor space. The living room and bedroom were combined, which Emma loved because she could lay in bed and watch TV, too. To her this was cool. It had a bed, small couch, and an old overstuffed chair. The bathroom was just big enough to hold a tub, toilet, and sink. That was the extent of her home in California. She didn't care. She kept it as spotless as was possible, and they weren't there that often anyway. Her work kept them gone most of the time during the week and on weekends, she tried to take Emma to the park as often as possible.

Tonight, Leslie was feeling worse as the evening wore on. She felt hotter and hotter and had developed a cough. After dinner, she usually gave Emma a bath and they would snuggle on the couch and watch a little TV before going to bed. That wasn't going to happen on this Friday night. She helped Emma put on her nightgown and got herself into a sweat suit that was an old favorite of hers.

After she got Emma settled with a cartoon, she decided to lie down for a while. The more she lay there, the worse she felt. Besides coughing and feeling hot, she was having trouble breathing. Feeling this bad, she was starting to get nervous thinking about how she was going to take care of her daughter. The way she felt, she couldn't imagine getting any better soon either. She remembered the card in her pocket that Jeff had given her. She didn't like to ask favors of anyone and the only reason she considered it now was Emma.

Fumbling around in her pocket, she found the card and called Jeff's cell phone number. He answered on the second ring.

"Jeff, this is Leslie Garrett. I'm so sorry to bother you."

"You're not bothering me at all, Leslie. What's the matter? Your voice sounds funny."

"That's because I'm really sick. I'm coughing, feel very hot, and am having trouble breathing. I'm scared because I don't think I can take care of Emma."

"Look, give me your address. We have a doctor who is an old family friend. I'll pick him up and be there right away."

After giving him the address, she went back to lay down. Every second that went by seemed like an eternity. Finally there came a knock at the door. She managed to get up to answer it.

CHAPTER 4

A

S SOON AS he got the call from Leslie, Jeff called Albert and told him to bring the car around. Then he called Doc and told him what was going on and that he'd pick him up on the way. Once they got on the way to East L. A., he thought of some of the questions he had for her. Why would a nice girl with a child want to live at the address she had given him? Why didn't she call an ambulance when she got sick? She must not know anybody here. He heard from staff at work that she didn't like to take help from people anyway.

When they got to her building, he told Albert to stay with the car and, he would call when he needed him.

Jeff and Doc got to the right apartment. Jeff knocked on the door, and when it opened found himself with Leslie in his arms as she passed out. After he laid her on the bed, Doc took over. Turning, he saw this little person with huge green eyes staring at him. Quickly, he picked up the little girl and took her to what he found to be the kitchen.

"What's your name?"

"Emma," she said with a quivering lip. Jeff realized she was trying to be brave and not cry.

"Emma, I'm here because your mommy called me and said she was sick. The man in there with her is a doctor. He'll take good care of her." Not really knowing how to take care of a child, he finally thought that if he could get her something to eat or drink, it would take her mind off her mother. "How about a glass of milk or a cookie?"

"No, I've already had my supper. I had chocolate cake."

"I like chocolate cake, too." Finally, they hit common ground. So began the conversation between a thirty-year-old man and a four-year-old girl over desserts until Doc called out to him to come into the living room.

Doc looked at Jeff with worry on his face and said, "She has pneumonia. We need to get her to the hospital right away."

"Look, Doc. Isn't there any other way to take care of this? If we take her to the hospital, what's going to happen to Emma?"

"Well, we can't leave her here. What else can we do?"

"What would they do for her in the hospital?"

"We'd give her antibiotics through an I. V. and put her on oxygen."

"Ok, this is going to sound crazy, but why couldn't we do that at my home?"

"Jeff, she's going to need twenty-four-hour nursing care, too."

"So. They have private-duty nurses I could hire."

Sighing, Doc said, "I know you well enough not to argue with you about this. I'll make some calls and get things set up. You call home and get things taken care of on your end." With that, Doc used his phone to get the nurses and equipment and medicine he would need.

At the same time, Jeff called his mother, explained what was going on and asked her to see that the suite next to his was made ready for Leslie and the room next to his parents was ready for Emma. If his mother was surprised at any of this, she didn't say anything. Jeff remembered that he had brought home a countless number of strays when he was a little boy. However, he had never brought home a stray human being. This was going to be interesting.

CHAPTER 5

AFTER SPEAKING TO his mother, Jeff called Albert and had him come to the apartment to help him. Returning to the kitchen, he sat down with Emma.

"Emma, you know your mommy is sick. She should go to the hospital, but I'm going to take you both to my house instead. Doc is going to take care of your mommy there."

"Will I get to be with Mommy?" Emma's voice sounded shaky and her eyes had gotten very wide.

"You can't stay in the same room, but I have a very pretty room for you. I think you'll like it. When Doc says it's ok, then you can go to your mommy's room and see her."

"Promise?"

"I promise. Pinky swear." As he and Emma crossed pinkys, Emma's face looked a lot less scared. "I need you to help me get your clothes packed. Do you have any suitcases?"

"Mommy keeps them under the bed." Taking his hand, she led Jeff to the living room. "Shh, Mommy's sleeping. Don't wake her."

Smiling at Emma (who by this time had stolen his heart), they quietly started packing clothes and anything else that they could get in the suitcases. By this time, Albert had gotten upstairs and Jeff let him in. After explaining what was going on, he introduced Albert to Emma.

"Doc, are you ready?"

"We're all set to go."

"Albert, can you take the suitcases?" questioned Jeff.

"No problem."

"Ok, then Emma, let's get your coat on and you hold Doc's hand so nothing happens to him. I'll carry Leslie."

After wrapping Leslie in a quilt he found on the bed, he picked her up and was surprised at how light she was.

They made a strange-looking group going down the stairs. Going down four flights was tough, but they finally made it to the car. Albert stowed the luggage in the trunk, while the rest got settled in the back of the limo. By this time, Emma was getting sleepy, and she laid her head against Doc and promptly fell asleep. During the drive home, Leslie did little more than cough and wheeze. She didn't even seem to sense that she wasn't in her own bed.

Wanting to know more about her illness, Jeff asked Doc how a cold can turn so quickly into pneumonia.

"There are a lot of things that can cause pneumonia, but I have a feeling that she hasn't been taking very good care of herself. She seems to be malnourished and, if she's like you, she works long hours. When she is home, I believe she spends more time taking care of her daughter and very little, if any, on herself."

Pulling into the garage, Emma woke up, stretched and rubbed her eyes. While Albert got the luggage out of the trunk, the others went into the kitchen. Doc and Jeff took Leslie upstairs to get settled in her room. Albert brought in the suitcases and took them upstairs.

"You must be Emma," said Mary. "We're Mary and Joe, Jeff's parents. This is Julia. She's going to take care of you while you're here."

Joe, trying to take her mind off her sick mother, said, "Emma, our cook, Mrs. O'Brien, made some chocolate chip cookies when she heard you were coming here. Would you like some cookies and milk?"

Emma answered, "Yes, Sir. Thank you."

"Good," said Joe, "because she wouldn't let me have any until you got here. And I really like chocolate chip cookies. Let's take your coat off and sit down. I think Julia is getting us those cookies."

CHAPTER 6

WHEN THEY GOT Leslie upstairs to her room, they found all the equipment that Doc had ordered and a nurse, Jennifer Rogers. Mrs. Rogers was in her mid-forties and had been a private-duty nurse for ten years. She loved taking care of people and was an efficient care-giver. She had all the equipment set up and the bed ready for Leslie.

Laying her gently on the bed, Jeff turned and saw that Albert had come in with the suitcases. Jeff indicated the one that was Emma's and asked Albert to take it down to her room. Then, looking through the other ones, he found a nightgown for Leslie. Giving it to Mrs. Rogers to put on Leslie, he discretely turned and talked to Doc about the care that was going to be needed. When Leslie was tucked comfortably in her bed, Doc had the nurse hook up the I. V. and oxygen.

After this was done, Doc talked to Jeff, "Her fever is the most urgent thing right now. It's high and we need to get that down. The antibiotics in the I. V. will help with that. The oxygen is going to help ease her breathing difficulties. It's just going to take time and good care. All the nurses come with good references so we won't have to worry about the care. We need to get that fever down. I'll stay the night to keep an eye on her. There's nothing else we can do now except watch her. Why don't you get some sleep? If I need something, I'll get you."

CHAPTER 7

JEFF DECIDED THAT he would go check on Emma before he went to his room. He saw his parents with Emma sitting at the table eating cookies and milk. "Is this party just for you three or can I join in?" he asked noticing that Emma had lost the worried look in her eyes.

"You can have some, Sir", she said to him. "Grandma and Grandpa said they can't eat any more."

Mary quickly spoke as she saw the puzzled look in her son's eyes, "Emma isn't allowed to call adults by their first name and we all decided that Mr. and Mrs. Harriman was way too much of a mouthful for her to say. The only thing we could come up with was Grandma and Grandpa. We couldn't come up with anything for her to call you. So you are 'Sir'."

"Well, I've certainly been called worse," laughed Jeff, munching on a cookie.

Julia came over just then and said, "I see a little girl who needs to get to bed. How would you like to go see your room and have a nice, warm bath?"

"Yes, please," said Emma, yawning.

"Have you ever had a sleep over?" asked Julia.

"I don't think so. What's that?"

"Well, I'll go get my pajamas and sleep in your room. We can talk a little bit and I can read you a story. My sisters and I used to do that a lot when we were young."

"That sounds like fun!"

Jeff smiled at Julia, gratefully. He hoped that she was going to keep Emma from being frightened in a strange house with strange people.

As Emma was starting to leave the room with Julia, she ran back to Jeff and said to him, "Sir, will you tell Mommy that I love her?"

"I certainly will. And don't forget my promise. You'll see your mommy when Doc says it's ok."

With the trust that only a child has, Emma turned and went off to have a fun-filled girls' night with Julia.

CHAPTER 8

J EFF TRIED TO sleep that night, but he kept wondering how Leslie was doing. At dawn, after tossing and turning, he got up, took a shower, and got dressed. Luckily he had no plans for this weekend, so he could devote all of his attention to his new guests.

He walked next door to check on Leslie first. Doc was still there and looked done in. The nurse had just finished checking Leslie's temperature.

Coming into the room, he asked Doc how things were going.

"Her temperature is down to 104," said the nurse.

Doc turned to Jeff and said, "That's the first time it's been down since we started the antibiotics. It's still going to be a while before she's feeling great, but at least we're going in the right direction. I think I'm going to go home now and get a few hours sleep. She's in good hands with her nurses and they all have my number. I'll be back this evening to check on her."

"Come on, Doc. I'll buy you a cup of coffee and some breakfast before you go."

"Now that's an offer I would be stupid not to take you up on. I never turn down anything from Mrs. O'Brien."

The rest of the weekend went by in a flash. Jeff kept busy sitting with Leslie and watching Emma win the hearts of everyone in the household. She loved to run and play outside, but he also noticed how excited she became when "Grandma" and "Grandpa" would read to her or take her out for ice cream. She also got to meet her new

"Aunts" Candace and Constance, Jeff's twin sisters. They told him they were a little shocked with the situation, but he noticed a change in their attitude after they met Emma. They both said to Jeff, "Since our children are older, it's wonderful to have a little one around again. We are going to spoil her, too."

Monday, Jeff went to work as always and explained Leslie's absence, omitting the fact that she was currently in his guest room. Everyone missed her and hoped that she would get well soon.

CHAPTER 9

B
Y MID-WEEK, LESLIE'S fever was down to an acceptable degree, and she was starting to wake up for short periods of time. The first time she can remember being awake, the surprise of looking around the room she was in was overwhelming. She asked the nurse the usual question: "Where am I?"

"You're in the guest room of Jeffrey Harriman. I'm Mrs. Eastbay and I'm happy that you're awake."

"Where's Emma?" This was more of a concern to her than her health or the fact that she was in Jeff's home. "Please, tell me."

"Now, don't worry. Mr. Harriman's parents took her shopping and to lunch."

"Why would they do that?"

"You will find out that around here your daughter is the light of everyone's life. Everyone loves her. Now you need to go back to sleep and start getting your strength back."

Believing the nurse that her daughter was all right and suddenly feeling very tired, Leslie closed her eyes and was asleep in about two seconds.

Getting home that evening, Jeff immediately went up to the room Leslie was in and found her sitting up in bed with Mrs. Rogers feeding her broth that Mrs. O'Brien insisted would do more good than all the medicine Doc would prescribe. She was still coughing and looking pale, but she did look better.

Seeing him in the doorway, she exclaimed, "I need to see Emma! I need to see my daughter! Please, Jeff."

Walking over to the phone, he hit the intercom button and found his mother. He asked her to bring Emma up to see her mommy. It didn't seem like any time at all that a whirlwind swept into the room screaming, "Mommy, Mommy. I have missed you so much." Leaping into Leslie's arms, she started crying. Leslie was already crying, and it was all anyone else in the room could do to not cry, too.

Finally, Emma pulled loose from her mom and ran over to Jeff and wrapped her arms around his legs. Looking up at him, with tears still in her eyes, she said, "Thank you, Sir. You kept your promise." Then she let loose of him and turned around and ran back to Leslie.

While they talked to each other, the rest of the people in the room left them alone. Soon, Emma was showing signs of sleepiness. She laid her head on Leslie's lap and fell asleep. It wasn't long after that when Julia came in and picked her up to take her to bed.

"We haven't met, Leslie, but my name is Julia and I've been nanny to this little tyke since she's been here. I must say she is a very well-mannered child, and the whole household loves her to pieces."

"Thank you, Julia, for taking such good care of Emma. She's all I have in the world, and I don't know what I would do without her. I'm also glad to know she's been so good. I try to teach her, but we don't always know how well kids do when they're not with you."

"Well, I'm going to put her to bed now. We're all glad that you're getting better. You'll be up and around before you know it."

"Thank you again, Julia."

CHAPTER 10

B Y THE TIME another week had gone by, Leslie (other than some coughing) was pretty much back to normal. She spent the week playing Go Fish and checkers with Emma. When Emma wasn't with her, she watched TV and slept. She only needed her day nurse and Mrs. O'Brien was filling her up with nutritious, yet light, food. Even tomorrow she wouldn't need the nurse at all. She was taking short walks on the balcony outside her room, and the fresh air felt wonderful to her.

On Saturday, after taking a shower and getting dressed, Leslie was eating a light lunch on the balcony, enjoying the beautiful weather. As she was finishing up with a cup of tea, Jeff came out to see her. They sat there chatting when Emma came running out with a bathing suit on. Julia was hurrying after her.

"Mommy, Mommy. Look at my new bathing suit," she said excitedly.

"It's very pretty, but where'd you get it?"

"Grandma and Grandpa bought it for me. Grandpa said that if I'm going to live here, I have to take swimming lessons."

"Come on, Emma," said Julia, "it's time for your lesson. You don't want to be late."

Leslie sat there, dumbfounded. She had already been told the story about the names, which she thought was very sweet. What she was shocked about was the fact that Emma thought they were going to live there and not go back to their apartment.

Quietly, Jeff said, "That's why I came up here to talk to you. I think Dad got ahead of himself. He didn't realize that I hadn't talked to you yet."

"Why would anyone think that we are going to live here?"

Trying to find the right words, he just decided to come right out with it and suffer the consequences. "I couldn't stand the thought of the two of you going back to that apartment. So I paid off your lease."

Not sure she heard him right, Leslie said, "I know you have done a nice thing for Emma and me and I owe you my life. But whatever would make you do such a thing without discussing it with me first? Why do you even think it would be appropriate for us to live here?" Suddenly, with eyes going wide, something awful came to mind. "What do you want from me to live here?"

Realizing what she was asking him, he hastily assured her. "You have to believe me. I don't want anything from you. I just wanted to help give you and Emma a better life. Everyone here has fallen so hard for Emma that they would be devastated if she left. And, one more thing. I'm engaged. So I wasn't trying to imply anything immoral. Please say yes. You both being here will certainly liven things up. I've never seen my parents act so young."

Surprised by the fact that Jeff was engaged, Leslie thought for quite a while on what to do. "Jeff, I can't afford to live here. I have certain financial obligations that just won't allow for it."

"I don't want any money from you. I don't normally talk about money, but I have enough to last me at least three lifetimes. I also believe that God gave me this money with the obligation to do good things with it. Haven't you ever prayed to God to help you and Emma? Well, maybe this is the help he wants you to have."

"Now, that's hitting below the belt. I don't like this, but I can see your point. We have a lot of details to sort out though. I'm not living here for nothing. I need to pay something."

"Before we decide on that, I have another question to ask you. You make a pretty good salary. Why are you in financial distress?"

Leslie couldn't hold back the tears when she thought of the answer to this question. Swallowing, she told him her story. "My husband and I married right out of high school. I worked while Troy went to college. Then I got pregnant and found out that Troy had cancer. When Emma was a year old, he died. If it hadn't been for her, I would have died, too. As if that wasn't bad enough, the medical bills started coming in. I could have declared bankruptcy, but somehow I just couldn't justify doing that. I contacted everyone I owed and told them that I would pay them if they would agree to work with me on the payments and not charge me any interest. They all agreed. I couldn't stand living in Ohio any longer, so I came out here to start a new life. That's why we were living where we were. It was all I could afford and still make payments to everyone."

"Leslie, I'm sorry I pried into your life. But, I think I can help you in a way that will let you keep your dignity. I'll have my secretary take care of your finances just like she does mine. We'll have your paycheck deposited in an account. Debra can take $150.00 a week out of that and pay me. That will cover food, utilities, nanny fees. I will advance you the money to pay off the medical bills, and you can pay me whatever you want every week. That solves everything, doesn't it?"

"Jeff, why are you doing all this for us?" questioned Leslie, with a tone of disbelief.

"Maybe it's just for some brownie points with the Big Guy upstairs. Have we got a deal?"

"Yes. Thank you. Now, I have a question for you."

"Fire away, Ohio."

"You said you're engaged. I've never heard about that. Tell me about it."

"Her name is Gwendolyn Parker. Her father is president of a very prestigious bank in L. A. I haven't seen her in a while, because she has been traveling in Europe with her parents for the last couple of months. I'll introduce you to her when they get back. By the way, I want you to make any changes to your room that you like."

Leslie thought about the room that Jeff had given her. The walls were a light mauve color with beautiful cherry woodwork. The furniture wasn't modern, and that suited her to a T. It was a huge room. In fact, it was bigger than her whole apartment. Yet, it had modern touches that were very nice – like a warm, gas fireplace in the living room area and large, flat-screen TVs in both the living room and bedroom. The bed was king-sized and so comfortable. The bathroom had a shower and a large soaking tub. It was a luxurious room and yet, it made her feel all warm and fuzzy. "No, Jeff. I can't think of any changes that I want to make."

"Let me know if you change your mind. Will you come down and join us for dinner tonight?" he asked.

"I'd like that."

"We'll be eating at seven. I'll come and take you down."

When he left, Leslie just folded. She put her head down on her arms and softly cried with tears of mixed emotions.

CHAPTER 11

WHEN JEFF CAME to get her for dinner, she was dressed in the nicest dress she had. She wanted to feel as good as possible, and that dress made her feel good. The dress hung on her because of her weight loss, but she was still a beautiful woman. Everyone could see that but her. She actually took his breath away when he saw her.

Since this was the first time she had been out of her room, Leslie was amazed at how beautiful the hallway was. It had rich, dark paneling and old family portraits, but it had the same homey feeling that her room had. When Jeff led her to a door that was actually the opening to an elevator, she was surprised. It was nice since she was still a little weak, and they were on the third floor. On the way down, Jeff told her a little bit about the house. His room and her room, along with two guest rooms, took up the third floor. His parents' room, Emma's room, and two guest rooms made up the second floor. The main floor had a living room, kitchen, dining room, office, and den.

"My great-grandfather had the house built after he married my great-grandmother. I've modernized it, somewhat, by merging small rooms to make larger rooms and updating bathrooms. But, I've tried to keep the integrity of the original house as much as possible. The house where Albert and his wife, Amy, live was once a carriage house. I did add on the garages though. And the kitchen is state-of-the-art," he told her with great pride in his voice.

Entering the dining room, Joe and Mary were already seated. Joe stood up when they came in, and Jeff held her chair for her. She was starting to feel like a real lady. Their manners were wonderful. She sat between Jeff and Joe and across from Mary. The room itself had the same woodwork as the rest of the house and was painted a soft grey color. The table, sideboard, and huge china cabinet were antiques. Above them was an intricate ceiling with a crystal chandelier that made the whole room sparkle. There were silver, brocade draperies hanging at the ceiling to floor windows at the end of the room. The original floors had been polished to a high gloss and showed off the excellent workmanship from his great-grandfather's day.

CHAPTER 12

WHILE THEY WERE eating dinner, Mary spoke to her. "We're so glad you have decided to stay with us. We have been having so much fun with Emma. Since she started her swimming lessons, she seems like a little fish. How do you like your room?"

"Well, Mrs. Harriman, I think it is the most beautiful room I've ever seen."

Joe spoke up quickly, "First of all, you must call us Joe and Mary. You and Emma are a part of our family now and we want you to feel a part of it. Secondly, I think it's time for dessert. What do you think, Leslie?"

Laughing, Leslie said, "I agree with you, Joe."

After dinner was over, Joe and Mary went to their room to watch TV before bedtime. Leslie said she wanted to say goodnight to Emma so Jeff took her to the second floor. He showed her his parents' room and then took her to Emma's room. Walking in, it was like going into a room made for a princess. Here instead of dark moldings, they were white and the walls were painted a pale shade of lavender. There was a white, canopied bed with lavender bedding and canopy. Even the carpeting and draperies were a pale lavender to match. The rest of the furniture was white.

Julia was in a rocking chair with Emma on her lap. They were reading a bedtime story. When Emma saw her mother, she ran over to her with obvious elation.

"Mommy, you've come to tuck me in." Then Emma ran over to the bed and crawled into it, so that Leslie could do just that.

Leslie tucked her in and said, "Sleep tight. Don't let the bedbugs bite. I love you, my sweet girl."

Giggling, Emma replied, "I love you, too, Mommy."

CHAPTER 13

L ESLIE WAS FEELING better every day. On Saturday evening, Jeff's twin sisters, Candace and Constance, and their husbands came to dinner. Jeff wanted them to meet Leslie and, of course, for Leslie to meet them. Mrs. O'Brien had served her wonderful pot roast, and everyone was having a good time chatting away.

In the middle of dinner, Anna Marie quietly told Jeff that he had a phone call. Since there were standing orders that dinner was not to be interrupted unless the call was important, he excused himself and left the table.

Picking the phone up in the den, a woman's voice said, "Hello, Jeffrey, darling. It's Gwendolyn."

"Gwendolyn, where are you?"

"I'm home. Father had to come home early for some business. We just got in a couple of hours ago. Why don't you come over here?" said Gwendolyn.

"I would love to, but I'm in the middle of dinner and my sisters are here. I really can't get away. Why don't you get in a cab and come on over and when we can leave, I'll take you home. There's someone here I want you to meet anyway."

"All right. I'll be right over," said Gwendolyn with an edge in her voice.

When Jeff got back to the table, he informed everybody of the conversation he had just had with Gwendolyn. Leslie noticed the sudden quiet and the looks between his sisters and their mother. She didn't think the men noticed, because they kept right on talking. Suddenly she was feeling very uncomfortable.

"Jeff, maybe I should go to my room. I'm sure that your fiancée won't want an outsider here on her first day home," said Leslie.

"Please, stay. I want her to meet you." Jeff didn't see a problem, but he was about to find out.

Greeting Gwendolyn with a kiss on the cheek, Jeff explained to her who Leslie was and why she was here. Gwendolyn was quiet while he was talking, but the fire in her eyes was unmistakable.

She said, "Jeffrey, I don't think it's a good idea for that woman and her child to be living here."

"I can assure you that nothing is going on between us. She's just someone who needs a little help, and that's what I'm doing," said Jeff, with a firmness that was unusual to him.

"We must not keep your family waiting any longer. We'll discuss this later," said Gwendolyn, also with a firmness to her voice.

CHAPTER 14

THE FAMILY HAD decided to have coffee and after-dinner drinks in the living room. Leslie could feel the coolness in the air when Jeff and Gwendolyn came in. The warmth which they had shown Leslie was not there when they greeted Gwendolyn. It didn't take her long to figure out why.

"Good evening, Miss Garrett. I'm Gwendolyn Parker, Jeffrey's fiancée." The voice was cool and clipped. "Jeffrey has informed me of your situation and that you are living with him now. Oh, and that you have a little girl."

Normally, Leslie would have smiled and let those remarks go, but something told her she'd better nip this in the bud. Smiling sweetly, she said, "Good evening, Miss Parker. I'm living in this house, but not WITH Jeff. And, yes, I DO have a wonderful little girl named Emma."

Leslie heard a snicker come from behind her, quickly covered up by a cough. She suspected it was Joe, but had a feeling it could have been any one of the family.

Suddenly feeling quite tired, Leslie decided to go to her room. She had had enough of Miss Parker. It took a while to go around the room to say good night to everyone. Finally she made her way upstairs.

Leslie got into her pajamas, washed her face, and brushed her teeth. As she was getting into bed, she thought again about Gwendolyn Parker. Somehow, she just couldn't figure out why Jeff was engaged to her. She certainly didn't seem like his type.

CHAPTER 15

SUNDAY, JEFF PLAYED golf with Gwendolyn, and Leslie and Mary lounged on the patio, while Joe and Emma played in the pool. It was a relaxing day for them all, except Jeff. Gwendolyn may have been "polite" when she met Leslie, but she was anything but that the whole eighteen holes of golf.

"Jeffrey, explain to me why that woman and her brat are living with you?" huffed Gwendolyn.

As patiently as possible, Jeff said, "I've already told you that I'm just trying to help a co-worker get back on her feet. When you say that she's living with me, that doesn't sound very nice. She's living in her own room in my home. The same as my parents. And please quit calling Emma a brat. She's a very sweet and well-mannered little girl. They are both staying where they are and that's that. Believe me, they are no threat to you." He put his arms around her and tried to give her a kiss. But, Gwendolyn pulled away from him. She didn't speak to him for the rest of the game.

By the time they got to the clubhouse, Jeff noticed that she had finally started to warm up and began talking to him again. He figured that she had decided to change tactics. After all, flies, and honey, and all that.

CHAPTER 16

LESLIE WAS RESTED when she got up Monday morning. She met Jeff at the car ready to go back to work. The money issues had been settled between them, and she was anxious to get back to her job.

When they got to the studio, everyone greeted her with a hug or kiss or both. They were glad to have her back. She was well liked, and they had all genuinely missed her.

Even though Leslie was glad to be back, it was a long day. Getting in the limo to go home, she told Jeff, "I certainly am going to get used to not having to drive back and forth to work. I'm exhausted. And I'm also relieved to know that Emma is being taken care of, and I don't have to worry about her."

Grinning, Jeff replied, "Please tell me you're not going to thank me every day, are you? You get a ride and my parents get to have fun with Emma. Now, help me go over my lines."

Giving a salute, she said, "Yes, Sir."

When they got home, Leslie went to Emma's room and kissed her good night and then went to her room. She went right to bed because she was so tired from her first day back.

CHAPTER 17

EVERYONE WAS GETTING settled into their own routine. The days were just flying by. Leslie was putting on some much-needed weight, and she was feeling wonderful. Emma was happy in her surroundings, and everyone else in the household was glad they were there. Thanksgiving was a happy occasion. Candace and Constance and their whole family came to the house. Even Gwendolyn seemed to be in a good mood. Her parents came for dinner. Leslie got along well with them. They were a lot like Mary and Joe. Emma got to stay up and eat with the kids.

After dinner, Leslie put Emma to bed. While she was tucking her in, Emma threw her arms around Leslie and said, "Mommy, I'm glad we live here. It makes me feel happy." Yawning, she closed her eyes and went to sleep.

Wiping the tears off her face, Leslie went back down to join the party.

After Thanksgiving was over, decorating for Christmas began. It took a lot of decorations for a house the size of the one they lived in. Everyone did their part. Mrs. O'Brien started baking and freezing goodies. It was Albert's job to do the outside decorating. Everyone else worked on the inside. Every day when Jeff and Leslie came home, there was something new to look at. Even Emma got to help. She colored Christmas pictures and Mary, Joe, and Julia helped her to cut out strips of red and green construction paper and make paper garlands. She also got to help put ornaments on the various trees that they put up in the house.

It was a festive household. Leslie, for the first time in years, was actually looking forward to the holiday. She went shopping and bought everyone in the house a gift. She even decided to get gifts for Gwendolyn and her parents. She got such joy from buying gifts for Emma this year. Christmas, in the past, had not been very joyful. With Troy gone and money being tight, they usually had a small holiday. But this year, she could afford (thanks to Jeff) to get Emma more than just a few pieces of clothing.

When Christmas Eve came, Emma was so excited. Julia helped her put out cookies and milk for Santa Claus. Mrs. O'Brien had even let Emma help her make them. Emma let Leslie put her to bed early, because she didn't want to take a chance on running into Santa. Leslie read her "Twas The Night Before Christmas."

When Emma went to sleep, Leslie went to her own room and gathered up the gifts she had purchased. She wanted to get them under the tree.

As she walked into the living room, she gasped when she saw the tree. She had never seen so many presents in her life. The tree was beautiful, and the gifts just made it look spectacular. When she put her packages under there, she noticed that most of them were for Emma.

Just then, Mary and Joe and Jeff came in. Turning to them with wide eyes, Leslie said, "You are all going to spoil her." They started to look a little guilty when she said, "But, I love you for it." With tears of joy in her eyes, she hugged each of them. "I've already been given my gift. A beautiful home and my new family."

On Christmas morning, when Leslie brought Emma downstairs, Jeff and his parents were waiting for them. After Emma had opened her gifts, Leslie passed out hers. She had gotten a locket for Mary with pictures of her children in it. Joe and Jeff got new watches which they both put on. Mary and Joe had gotten Leslie a beautiful nightgown with matching robe and slippers. Then Jeff gave her a necklace with her birthstone (an opal) hanging from the chain. She had never seen a more lovely and delicate piece of jewelry.

They were all thanking one another, when Jeff told Emma that Santa Claus had left her one more gift, and it was outside on the patio.

Making her close her eyes, they all went out to see this last gift. Leslie almost lost it when she saw what it was. It was a miniature car, just Emma's size. Jeff took a squealing Emma over to show her how to operate the car. All Leslie could do was shake her head and laugh.

As Emma took off in her new car, Jeff came back to the others. Smiling sheepishly, he looked at Leslie. "I just couldn't resist."

Again, all Leslie could do was laugh at him. He looked like such a little boy.

When they managed to get Emma out of her car, they all went in to have Christmas breakfast together. Mrs. O'Brien had outdone herself. Jeff always tried to give her the day off, but she insisted that nobody was making Christmas breakfast for them except her. Dishes of eggs, sausage, bacon, biscuits and gravy, pancakes, and pecan waffles were already lined up on the sideboard. There was also plenty of fruit, coffee, and tea. She said to them, "If anyone goes hungry, it won't be my fault."

After breakfast, Julia took Emma back outside to play with her car, Mary and Joe went to their room to take a much needed nap. Leslie decided to rest in her room, too. One of her gifts was a book and she wanted to get started reading it. Jeff went up to take a shower and get ready to go to Gwendolyn's for the day. Her parents were having their annual Christmas party for family and important customers of the bank. He wouldn't be back until late. Mary and Joe would be having dinner at the home of Constance and her family.

Emma drove her car around until both she and Julia were ready to drop. By that time, Leslie had been watching them from the patio. She was enjoying every minute of it. When driver and the chaser finally came back to the house, Leslie took Emma in to get some dinner while Julia put the car in its special place that had been made in the garage. Leslie then made Julia take the rest of the evening off. Leslie and Emma sat in the kitchen and ate the leftovers that Mrs. O'Brien had for them in the refrigerator. Then Leslie gave Emma her bath and put the happy little girl to bed. Leslie then went back to read some more of her book. When Jeff came upstairs after a boring day at Gwendolyn's, he found Leslie in her chair, fast asleep. Taking the book off her lap, he covered her with an afghan and went to bed.

CHAPTER 18

THE WEEK AFTER Christmas, the household was busy getting ready for the Harriman's annual New Year's Eve party. They went all out for this gala event. All of the family would be there along with all of the employees. There would be a band set up on a platform over the pool, and the best caterer would serve the best food. Leslie was feeling uncomfortable because there would be over two hundred people at the party, and she wasn't used to being in the company of that many people. She couldn't even use Emma as an excuse because Emma was going to be at Candace's house with a babysitter for a couple of days.

The day of the party was a flurry of people setting up for the evening. The band was setting up their equipment outside. The caterers were busy setting up drink and food stations, inside and out, and wonderful smells were coming from the kitchen.

Leslie had bought a little black dress for the occasion and was putting the finishing touches on her makeup when Jeff knocked on her door.

"Come in," she said.

Jeff opened the door and started to say something. Then Leslie turned around and he said instead, "Wow, you look beautiful!"

"Are you sure I look ok for this party?" Leslie said anxiously.

"You certainly do. I don't think you've ever looked better," Jeff said. "I just stopped in to escort you downstairs. And Leslie, I really want you to have a good time tonight. They'll be plenty of people you know. Can you try?"

"Yes, I will. I promise," Leslie answered. "I'm ready. Let's go down."

The party was in full swing and everyone, including Leslie, was having a great time. They were eating and drinking and dancing and just standing around talking to one another.

Leslie decided to take a short walk to get some fresh air. As she sat down on one of the many benches that were scattered around the property, a man came out of the trees.

Seeing him, Leslie jumped up and gave a small squeak.

The man put up his hands as if to push her and quickly said, "I'm sorry. I didn't mean to scare you. I was just taking a walk. I'm guessing that you were doing the same thing. My name is Walter Jackson."

"Oh, Mr. Jackson. I recognize you now. Yes, you did scare me. I thought I was alone. I'm Leslie Garrett." Leslie's heart was still beating wildly. She knew who he was. She had seen many of his movies. He was a very popular actor, and he wasn't bad to look at, either.

"Please call me Walt. How about we sit down?" The sound of her voice made him want her to keep talking. "I know why I'm out here. Why are you?"

"You can call me Leslie. I was just getting some fresh air. It was getting close to midnight and I didn't want to be inside with everyone."

"Aren't you with someone?" he inquired.

"No, I'm not. What about you?"

"No, I'm currently alone." Just then they heard a lot of noise coming from the house. Looking at his watch, Walt said, "Well, it's midnight. Since we're both alone would it be all right if I gave you a New Year's kiss?" Not giving her time to answer, he leaned toward her and lightly gave her a kiss on the lips.

For the second time that evening, Leslie was startled. She hadn't been kissed like that since her husband died.

Trying to cover over the awkward silence, Walt said, "Now it's officially the new year."

Recovering from the kiss, Leslie replied, "Yes, it is. We did have to make it official, didn't we?"

Walt said to her, "I'd like to know you better. Would you let me take you to dinner Saturday?"

Leslie was in a quandary about the question. Not only had she not been kissed since her husband died, she had not been on a date since then. She didn't feel ready for dating, yet he seemed so nice that it might be interesting to go to dinner with him. So she agreed to dinner and gave him her number so that he could call her with the details.

Standing up, Walt said, "I have to get up early tomorrow, so I have to leave now. May I walk you to the house? I don't feel comfortable leaving you out here by yourself."

"Thank you. That would be nice." Instead of taking her hand, he offered her his arm. Leslie liked this and thought of him as a real gentleman. So she took it, and they walked slowly to the house.

CHAPTER 19

THE NEXT DAY everyone slept in, and the house was abnormally quiet. Even Mrs. O'Brien wasn't in her kitchen until 8 o'clock. Finally, people started drifting down for coffee and tea. Tradition was that everyone snacked on food left over from the night before. Jeff and Leslie found themselves alone together out on the patio. Leslie decided to take this opportunity to ask him about Walter Jackson.

"Jeff, I wanted to ask your opinion about something," said Leslie cautiously.

"Of course, anything."

"I was talking to Walter Jackson last night, and he asked me out to dinner. You know I haven't been out since my husband died and, quite frankly, I don't know what to do. What kind of a guy is he? Do you think I should go?" asked Leslie.

Jeff took a moment to think about her questions and said, "I've known Walt since we were boys. He's a good man. I think that for your first time out, he would be a good fit for you. You wouldn't have to worry about him trying anything. It's been three years. Don't you think it's time for you to start dating again?"

"I guess it probably is. It just seems so strange to be even considering it. I suppose you're right. After all, it's just dinner. If I don't like it, I don't have to do it again," said Leslie with more confidence than she felt.

"That's true. It's only dinner."

Later that day, Walt called Leslie and thanked her for a nice evening. They settled on plans for dinner on Saturday.

CHAPTER 20

SATURDAY CAME UPON Leslie fast. Walt had said not to dress up because they had decided to go to a little restaurant he knew. So she showered, put on her makeup, and got into a pair of dressy jeans with a red sweater she had gotten for Christmas.

Ready to go, she stopped by Emma's room to kiss her good night. Emma and Julia were putting together a jigsaw puzzle of a kitty. They both looked up when Leslie walked into the room.

Julia smiled at her and said, "You look lovely, Leslie."

Emma added in, "Yes, Mommy. You look so pretty."

"Thanks to both of you. I came in to get my good night hug and kiss from you, Emma."

At that, Emma got up and ran over to Leslie and put her arms around her legs. Looking up, she said, "I love you, Mommy. I hope you like your dinner."

"I'm sure I will, sweetie. You behave for Julia."

"I will, Mommy. Good night."

"Good night, Julia. I have my phone if you need me," said Leslie.

"Good night, Leslie. I'm sure we'll be just fine. Have a good time," said Julia.

CHAPTER 21

WALT PULLED UP to the gate and pressed the intercom button. He was let in and pulled up to the front door. It opened before he could even ring the bell. Anna Marie let him in. She told him, "Leslie is on her way down, Mr. Jackson. Please come in."

At that moment, he looked up and saw Leslie walking toward him. As she reached him, she smiled shyly and said, "Hello, Walt. Am I dressed ok for dinner?"

Looking her over with admiration in his eyes, Walt said, "Yes, just fine. We're going to a restaurant that belongs to a friend of mine. I think you'll enjoy it."

"Well, let's get going then."

When they got to the restaurant, they seated Walt and Leslie at Walt's usual table in the far corner. After they placed their order, the owner came over and greeted them. He was a big man and very happy. He reminded Leslie of Santa Claus in street clothes. After that, the waiter brought over a bottle of Walt's favorite wine.

Leslie checked out her surroundings noticing the aged, flowered wallpaper and that the hanging plants were real and well-loved. The tables and chairs were of a vintage variety with beautiful lace table cloths. "Walt, this place is so homey. I just love it!" said Leslie.

"I was hoping you would. Now I'd like to get to know you better. Tell me about yourself."

Leslie knew this was coming. She reminded herself that she was an adult and could get through this. She braced herself and said, "I come from Ohio and have been here about nine months." As she continued on with her story, including how she came to be living in Jeff's house, she felt herself relaxing.

When she finished she saw, not pity, on Walt's face, but admiration. He said, "You are one amazing woman. What you have gone through would have broken so many people, but not you. You seem to have bounced back. I have to admire you. That must have taken a lot of courage to put your daughter first and live at Jeff's. It also doesn't surprise me that he and his family are embracing you the way they have. They are good people."

Leslie said, with relief, "I want to hear about you now."

"I certainly can't top your life. In fact, it's really pretty dull. I grew up in a loving family with an older brother and a younger sister. My father is a financial consultant, and my mother stayed at home to take care of us. My brother went to work with my father, and that's what I was supposed to do. However, being the rebel that I am, I took up acting. I think I've done all right in the industry. I live by myself. I have Charlie, who takes care of everything in the house. I would be lost without him. I'd also have to eat out every day and live in a pig sty. That's my boring life."

"It sounds normal to me, not boring. Here's my take on you. You love your family, your job, and your life. Am I right?" asked Leslie.

Grinning sheepishly, Walt answered, "Yes, you're right. I do love all those things. But I am also going to 'love' getting to know you better."

Their order came to the table just then. As they ate, they both said how good it was and kept up a running conversation, too. They dawdled over their espressos and continued to find new things to talk about. All of a sudden, they noticed that there were no more customers in the restaurant. Looking at his watch, Walt said, "I can't believe it's after midnight. I think we'd better leave before we get thrown out."

Leslie agreed and said, "I need to get home anyway. But I've had a good time."

Walt paid the bill, took Leslie's arm, and escorted her to the car.

When they got to Leslie's home, she handed Walt her card to open the gate. When they got to the house, Walt helped her out of the car and walked her up to the door.

Turning to him, Leslie said, "Thanks for a wonderful evening. Honestly, I didn't expect to have so much fun. I was quite nervous, but you made me feel comfortable."

"Well, I'm glad for that. That will make the next time easier. How about next Saturday?"

"Okay, I'd like that."

Kissing her lightly on the cheek, Walt turned and got in the car. Waving, he drove off.

Leslie watched him until he turned onto the street. Then she went in the house, checked on Emma, and went to bed.

CHAPTER 22

WHILE LESLIE WAS having dinner with Walt, Jeff was at the opera with Gwendolyn. On the drive there, she was telling him (for the hundredth time, at least) that he needed to get Leslie and Emma out of his house.

"I'm telling you, Jeffrey, it just isn't proper for them to be there. People are going to think that you're sleeping with her. I'm trying to believe that you aren't, but I'm starting to have my doubts about that," said Gwendolyn, heatedly. Albert, who was driving them in the limo, looked up in the rear view mirror at that moment. He rolled his eyes as he caught Jeff looking at him. Jeff hastily looked away and stifled a grin.

"Gwendolyn, we've been over this too many times. I am not sleeping with Leslie. I am not going to kick them out of my house. You just need to deal with those facts. Can you please let it go? I'd like to enjoy my time with you and the opera." Jeff was disgusted with the conversation topic and wondered when she was going to stop talking about it.

At intermission, Gwendolyn seemed to be in a better mood. While they enjoyed their champagne, they mingled with other guests. They saw many of Gwendolyn's friends and those of her parents.

After the opera was over, they went back to spend the rest of the evening with Gwendolyn's parents. Jeff usually enjoyed these evenings. Somehow, tonight, it was a little boring.

Making an excuse about having to get up early the next day, Jeff went home. He was restless and decided to have a drink in his room. He poured himself a scotch and sat down to read some scripts. After a while, he heard Leslie's bedroom door open and close. Suddenly, he was really tired and went to bed. What a strange evening.

The next morning at breakfast, Emma asked Leslie if she had a good time on her date.

Leslie said, "Yes, it was very nice." She went on to tell Emma, Jeff, Joe, and Mary about the evening. Although there were plenty of comments and laughter, Jeff was quiet. No one seemed to notice this except Joe.

CHAPTER 23

THE WINTER WENT on as normal. Leslie and Jeff went to work. Leslie went on dates with Walt. They went to the movies, dinner, museums. They also went to his house to watch TV and eat Charlie's wonderful cooking. Walt came to Leslie's for dinners, too. Jeff went to the ballet and the opera with Gwendolyn. They, too, ate dinner at her house and his. Emma continued to enjoy her new life with lots of loving people.

It was finally getting toward the end of the shooting season for Jeff's TV show. One day Leslie was bringing Jeff a cup of coffee when she overheard an argument between Jeff and another man.

"Franklin, you are totally out of line. I can't have you going around telling people about the show's scripts before the show has aired. I don't care if it is only your family. Word had gotten out and it's ruining things. A lot of people depend on this job and if the show gets cancelled, it'll be your fault. You're fired!" screamed Jeff. Leslie had never seen Jeff this angry before, but she understood that he was thinking of the rest of the cast and crew, not himself.

"Jeff, can't you give me another chance? I promise not to do it again," pleaded Franklin.

"No, I can't. I don't trust you anymore. Get out now," said Jeff. He had calmed down somewhat, but he was still angry.

"You're going to regret this, MR. Harriman. You haven't seen the last of me yet," said Franklin. He then stomped off the set.

Turning, Jeff saw Leslie with his coffee. "Thanks, Leslie, I really need this now. I assume you heard all that?"

"Yes, I did. I don't see how you had any choice in the matter. You're right. A lot of people depend on this job. But, what about his threat? Aren't you concerned about it?"

"No, he just needed something to say in the heat of the moment. He's gone now. So, let's get back to work." At that, he handed back the empty cup and turned to talk to the director. Leslie took the cup back and went back to her work, too.

They both soon forgot about the incident.

CHAPTER 24

THE LAST DAY of shooting for the season was here. It was always a bittersweet day for everyone. People were looking forward to vacations, but sad at not seeing friends, who were like family, until the start of the next season. And, there was always the chance that the show could get cancelled before the next season started. It wasn't likely, because ratings had never been higher, but one never knew.

They were finishing up on small details, and catering was getting ready for the wrap party. Jeff and Leslie were standing together when Jeff realized that he had forgotten his wallet in his trailer.

Leslie said, "I'll go get it for you. Where is it?"

"You don't have to get it. I can go myself," he said.

"No, you should stay here. I'll just be a minute."

"All right. It's on my dresser," Jeff said.

"Ok. Be right back," Leslie said as she walked toward the door.

As Leslie went to Jeff's trailer, she was thinking about Emma. Walt had gone out of town on location for a couple of months so she was going to take Emma to the zoo.

She opened the door and started walking to the bedroom when she heard a click. She turned around slowly and stared into the eyes of Franklin. He had a wild look about him, and the thought came to her that he was high on drugs.

"Well, well. What have we here?" said Franklin, with a crooked grin on his face. "I came here looking for MR. Harriman, but I found someone even better."

Trying to stay calm, Leslie said, "Franklin, I think you should get out of here and off the lot. You know you aren't supposed to be here." As she said this, Leslie was trying to casually look for the phone and something she could use as a weapon.

As he slowly walked toward her, Franklin said, "MS. Garrett, what's better than getting revenge on a person?"

Trying to keep him talking, Leslie replied, "I don't know. What's better than getting revenge on a person?"

"Getting revenge by killing someone that that person cares for."

Leslie was starting to shake inside and had grown cold, realizing what Franklin meant. She lunged for the telephone. As she tried to grab it, Franklin jumped forward and pulled it out of her hand and the connection out of the wall. Screaming, she tried to get away from him, but Franklin was much too fast for her.

He was so powerful. She couldn't get out of his grasp, but she kept on screaming. He threw her across the room where she hit a wall and slid down to the floor. He had knocked the breath out of her, and as he jumped over the sofa to start beating on her with his fists, she was unable to move. She still tried to scream, but it wasn't coming out of her mouth very loudly. He picked her up again and threw her into the TV set. She was almost unconscious when he suddenly pulled out a knife. She couldn't move, and all that went through her mind was that Emma was going to be an orphan. Tears were rolling down her face as he sliced her belly. Then there was nothing but blackness.

As Franklin was about to go in for the kill, the door was slammed open and there were two guards with pistols drawn. They yelled at Franklin to put down the knife. He turned to them, but turned back to Leslie to plunge the knife into her. The guards fired into him and finally brought him down. Just then, Jeff darted into the room and ran to Leslie. Carefully, he cradled her in his arms and yelled for someone to call 911. He also yelled for towels. He then put the towels over her to try and stop the bleeding. As he did this, he kept talking to her.

"Come on, Ohio, stay with me, sweetheart. You're strong and I'm not going to let you die. Fight for Emma and everyone who loves you."

They continued to bring towels to him, and he was still trying to stop the blood flow, all the while murmuring to her. Finally the paramedics got there. They got her into the ambulance with Jeff right behind them. As they were leaving, the police showed up and entered the trailer.

CHAPTER 25

WHEN THE AMBULANCE got to the hospital, the paramedics were getting Leslie into a trauma room as fast as they could. Jeff tried to go in with her, but a nurse closed the door on him. He just stood there trying to comprehend the situation. She couldn't die! That would be too cruel. He thought of Emma and what would happen to her if … No, he couldn't think that way. She was going to be fine. He had to believe that.

Just then, a woman with a name tag, took his arm and said, "Mr. Harriman, my name is Lucille Twilling. I'm a patient liaison, and I need you to come with me now. Please, Mr. Harriman. I need to take you to a private waiting room to keep you away from the press. They monitor police calls, and they'll be here soon." There was an urgency in her voice and it brought him out of his reverie.

Tugging at his arm, she led him up to the private room. She poured him a cup of coffee and had him sit down so she could talk to him.

"Mr. Harriman, is there someone I can call for you? Ms. Garrett's family or any friends?"

Jeff was still in a daze and as he looked down at his blood-soaked clothes, he said, "No. She has no family other than a five-year-old daughter. My family is the only one she has. I need to call my parents so they can keep Emma from finding out about her mother."

"While you're doing that, I'll call down and see what I can find out about Ms. Garrett." Lucille was very efficient in her job. It was her duty to keep calmness in situations like this. And this one was bad. For the sake of Leslie's daughter, she hoped there was a happy ending. From what she had seen and heard, it wasn't looking like there was going to be a positive ending to this.

Finding his phone, Jeff dialed his home phone. When his father answered, Jeff almost broke down. Gathering his composure, he said, "Dad, Leslie's been hurt."

Joe interrupted his son, saying, "Yes, Jeff, your mother heard about it on the news. We were hoping you would call soon and let us know what was going on."

"Dad, you've got to make sure that Emma doesn't hear about it."

"Your mom is taking care of that. We are all keeping her away from TV and the radio. Don't worry about that. You know we'll protect her. Now tell us about Leslie. The news report said that Leslie's injuries were severe."

"I'm not sure about all that happened. I just know that she was knifed. She was bleeding so hard and I couldn't stop it." Jeff was starting to get hysterical and knew that wouldn't help. Taking a deep breath, he continued, "She's in the hospital now. I'm with a Lucille Twilling. She's trying to find out information for me. Dad, I need a change of clothes. Can you have Mom pack a suitcase with some things for me for a few days? She'll know what to pack. I'm not leaving here until Leslie's better."

"I will, Son. I'll have Albert bring it to you," said Joe.

"Dad," Jeff said, trying to keep the tears from coming.

"Yes?"

"It was my fault she was hurt."

"How could it have been your fault?" said Joe, unbelieving.

"I forgot my wallet and she went to get it for me. If I had gone for it myself, she would be ok now." This time he couldn't stop the tears.

"Jeff, we've always told you that things happen for a reason, and it's not for us to question that. Just be in a positive mood and believe that she's going to be all right. Can you do that?" said Joe, trying to keep his emotions from showing in his voice.

"Yes, I can. Thanks, Dad. I love you. Mom, too. I'll call you as soon as I know anything. And have Albert ask for Lucille Twilling at the desk."

"Good-bye, Son."

CHAPTER 26

AFTER TALKING TO his dad, Jeff turned to Lucille to see what she had found out about Leslie.

Lucille said, "Leslie is in surgery, but that's all I know at this time."

Just then, the door opened and Doc came in. "Jeff, I got here as soon as I could. Do you know anything yet?"

"No, just that she's in surgery," replied Jeff.

Doc asked Lucille, "Who's the surgeon?"

"Dr. Johnson."

Doc said, "Well, that's great. Jeff, he's one of the best surgeons in the country. Leslie's in good hands. She's a fighter – you know that."

So they waited. Jeff finally started pacing. It wasn't too long before Lucille got a call that Albert was there. She had someone bring him up to the room. When he got there, he greeted Doc and Lucille. Then he went to Jeff and, in spite of the bloody shirt, wrapped Jeff in a big bear hug. Albert had known Jeff since Jeff was a kid and knew he was hurting.

"Here's some things from your mom. I brought food and coffee from Mrs. O'Brien. Mary also sent Emma's picture that Leslie kept on her night table and the quilt from her bed. She thought it might help."

"Thanks, Albert. This means a lot. Give everyone my thanks. I know they're praying for Leslie. Just be careful around Emma. We can't let her know anything yet," said Jeff gratefully.

"Don't you worry about Emma. She went to Constance's house for dinner and to spend the night. She'll stay there for as long as need be."

"I should have known that things would be taken care of at home. I'll call as soon as I know anything. Again, tell everyone thanks. Let me change clothes and you can take these home. Mrs. O'Brien would have a fit if I didn't send them back." Lucille handed him a hospital bag for his clothes, and he went into the bathroom to change. When he was finished, he handed the bag to Albert, who said his good-byes and left.

"Jeff, you should make arrangements for Leslie's room and nursing care. Do you want the same nurses you had the last time?" asked Doc.

"Yes, I would. And the best private room available," said Jeff.

"I'll take care of it with Lucille." Doc went over to Lucille to give her the information she needed to put everything in place. Jeff got up to look out the window while he waited for news on Leslie. When Doc had finished talking to Lucille, he went to Jeff, squeezed his shoulder and said, "I'll keep in touch about Leslie, but, right now, I have to go. Chin up, Jeff."

Arrangements had been completed for Leslie's care, but it was still another two hours before the phone rang. Lucille answered it and said, "Yes." She listened for a few moments, then said, "I understand. Thank you."

Smiling, she said to Jeff, "Ms. Garrett came through surgery and Dr. Johnson will be in shortly to give you more details."

Feeling like an incredible weight had been lifted from his shoulders, Jeff said, "Thank you, God."

It was only a few moments before Dr. Johnson came in to talk to them. Removing his surgical hat, he sat down and addressed Jeff, "Mr. Harriman, as you know, Ms. Garrett has come through surgery. She's in recovery right now and will be there about an hour. In addition to a lot of abrasions and contusions, she has three fractured ribs. The slice to her abdomen caused a lot of bleeding which required some transfusions, but luckily no organs were hit. The concern now is her concussion. Her head was hit pretty hard, and that's what we need to watch. The next forty-eight hours are crucial. I assume Lucille has her room arrangements made." With that statement, he looked over at Lucille, who nodded. "She'll go from recovery to her room. You may go there and wait on her, if you'd like. I'll be checking on her regularly. Do you have any questions for me?"

Breathing easier, Jeff said, "Not at this time, anyway. Thank you, Doctor, for all you've done."

"It makes my job better when my patients are fighters, like her. I'll see you later." Dr. Johnson left and both Jeff and Lucille got up.

Lucille said, "Let me take you to her room."

Entering Leslie's room, Jeff saw that it was a bright and cheery place to recover. He thanked Lucille for all her help.

Before she left, she said, "Here's my card. If you need anything, please don't hesitate to call me. I'm sure everything will be better now."

CHAPTER 27

I T WAS ANOTHER hour before they brought Leslie back to her room. It had been arranged that Leslie would have the same nurses she had before when she was sick. Jeff was glad because he knew that familiar faces would speed up her recovery and ease her mind.

The nurse had told Jeff that Leslie was going to look rough when she came in, but it was still a shock when he saw her. She looked so little, almost child-like. She was very pale and had cuts and bruises all over her face and arms, which was all he could see. She was so quiet that he got closer to make sure she was breathing. When the nurse got her settled and checked her oxygen and I.V., he brought up a chair as close to the bed as possible. He wanted to be able to face her so he could talk to her.

He had already put Emma's picture on the night table, and now he took her quilt and draped it across her bed. He leaned over and kissed her cheek, then settled into the chair to read to her. He had heard that even people who were in a coma could hear you. So reading it was.

Jeff had been reading for a few hours, and his voice was starting to sound rough and ragged. He got up, stretched, and went to the bathroom. He took a quick shower while he was in there. That rejuvenated him enough so that he could keep going. After pouring another cup of coffee, he sat back down and decided to talk to Leslie for a while.

The nurses took Leslie's vitals every fifteen minutes, and everything looked good there. The doctor had also been in to check on her incision and the rest of her injuries. He said, "Everything is what I expected."

When the nurse saw Jeff with another cup of coffee, she went to the refrigerator and made him a plate of food.

As she put the plate out for him, she said, "Mr. Harrington, you are going to eat this food and rest for a while or I'm going to make you go home."

He said, as he took the plate, "You would, too. Ok, I'm eating."

He had to admit to himself that the food did make him feel better. After that, he sat back down, tilted the chair back, took Leslie's hand and started talking to her softly. "I know you need time to heal, so you take that time. But I'm not going anywhere. When you wake up, I'll be here."

Jeff managed to get a few hours of sleep, which after the stress of the day before, he really needed. When he woke, there had been no change in Leslie's condition. So he started to read to her again. A routine began – vitals' checks, coffee, doctor checking in, more vitals' checks. But Leslie still had not awakened. Jeff kept in touch with his parents.

Mary put Emma on her lap and said, "Your mommy isn't feeling very good. She had to go to the hospital for a little bit so she could feel better."

Emma asked her, "Is Sir with her?"

Mary said, "Yes. Since Mommy can't take you to the zoo, Aunt Constance and Uncle John are going to. They, also, want you to stay with them for a few days."

Sadly, Emma said, "Sir will take care of Mommy. I know that. I'll have fun with Aunt Constance and Uncle John, but I wish Mommy could have taken me."

Joe said, "We all do, honey. We all do."

CHAPTER 28

I T WAS ABOUT nine o'clock on Saturday night when Jeff's phone rang. He saw that it was Gwendolyn. Sighing, he got up to be able to talk to her in private. Answering, he said, "Hello, Gwendolyn."

"Where the hell are you, Jeffrey?" said Gwendolyn, in a fit of rage.

"I'm at the hospital with Leslie. I called you and told you what happened." He was trying to be as patient as possible. But, he was tired, and he didn't need this.

"You're STILL there? You were supposed to be here for my parents' dinner party. Have you been there with her since the accident? I can't believe you're being so inconsiderate to me."

"Yes, I'm STILL here. She's still in a coma and we don't even know if she's going to come out of it. Somehow, your party just doesn't seem very important to me right now." Jeffrey finally had had enough. The straw had broken the camel's back, the frosting was on the cake, and the cherry was on the sundae. He blew his top – in a gentlemanly fashion, of course. "Gwendolyn, I can't take you one minute longer. You are the most obnoxious, inhuman, unkind, selfish bitch I have ever known. You have given me nothing but grief since you got home from Europe. I am sick and tired of it. I am calling off our engagement. I could never marry you. I wish you nothing but happiness, but it's not going to be with me. We would never be happy together. So find someone else who will let you lead him around by a leash. Good-bye, Gwen." With that, Jeff disconnected the call. Suddenly he felt so free.

He went back to Leslie and continued to read. For the first time since he became engaged to Gwendolyn, he had hope for a good life.

CHAPTER 29

I T WAS ONE o'clock Sunday afternoon. It was forty-four hours since the 'incident', as the beating of Leslie came to be known. Jeff was still in contact with his parents (although he didn't tell them about his confrontation with Gwendolyn) and had also talked several times with Walt, who was still on location.

Jeff was still sitting by Leslie's bed, holding her hand and reading to her in his hoarse voice. He was having a hard time holding his emotions in check since the forty-eight-hour deadline was coming up soon.

Suddenly he felt the hand in his move. He looked up at Leslie and saw a tear running down her cheek. The nurse immediately started to take Leslie's vitals.

Trying to stay calm, Jeff gently said, "Leslie, open your eyes. Everything's ok. Just open your eyes, honey. Please."

Slowly, Leslie opened her eyes and looked around. She was afraid that her attacker was there in the room. "Where..is..he?" she asked.

"He's not here, Leslie." He wasn't sure how much he should tell her. "He can't hurt you anymore."

"But, he could come back," she cried.

"No. He can't." Jeff had to tell her. "He's dead. When the guards came into the trailer, he wouldn't stop. When he started going toward you again, they shot him. He was so high on drugs that it's possible he didn't even know what he was doing."

Leslie was slowly gathering her thoughts together. Finally, she said, "He was after you. He said I was the next best thing. Killing me would hurt you. So it was the same thing – even better."

"I'm sorry, Leslie. If I would have known, I would have never let you walk into that." The guilt Jeff was feeling went so deep, he didn't know if he could ever get over it.

"Of course, you wouldn't have. But, you wouldn't have either. You would have called the police." They both started laughing, but Leslie stopped at once and started moaning. "Jeff, what's wrong with me?"

Just then the doctor walked in. "Hello, Ms. Garrett, I'm Dr. Johnson. I'm glad to see that you are awake. Can you tell me what you're feeling?"

Slowly, Leslie said, "I have a headache. My ribs hurt. My abdomen hurts. I feel achy all over. I don't feel like I have any strength and I'm very tired."

Dr. Johnson gave her his best doctor's smile as he said, "All those things are typical of what you're here for. Good, no surprises. Your head hurts because you have a concussion. Your ribs hurt because three of them are fractured. Your abdomen hurts because you were stabbed. And the rest is because you were beaten up by a man high on drugs." Leslie was shocked at his honesty and her blood pressure had risen because of it. Jeff and the nurse were both holding one of her hands and trying to soothe her.

Dr. Johnson continued, "Ms. Garrett, you needed to know what was wrong with you, and I don't believe in sugar-coating anything. Your head is getting better. Your ribs are going to be sore for a while. The oxygen will help you to breathe easier. We operated on you to close the wound. Luckily no vital organs were hurt. You'll have a scar, but you'll heal. The cuts, scratches and bruises are already starting to get better. Do you have any questions for me?"

"No, I don't think so. Except, when can I go home? My little girl must be really upset by now." Leslie was only half kidding Dr. Johnson.

"Ms. Garrett, it's been less than forty-eight hours since they brought you in. I think you may have to wait a few days before we can even consider it. But, I admire the fact that you even asked. You're a fighter and that's what helped save your life. Now, I want to look at your incision and see how that's coming along."

Jeff said, "I'm going to call home and let everyone know you're awake. They've been waiting for this call."

"Does Walt know what's happening?"

"Yes, I've talked to him several times. He wanted to be here, but he can't leave the shoot. I'll call him, too," said Jeff.

"Thanks."

As Jeff went into the other room to make his calls, the doctor took off the dressing to check her. Leslie was again shocked at how long the incision was, but Dr. Johnson reassured her that it was healing well.

"Considering everything you've gone through, you are coming along very well," said Dr. Johnson. "The nurse is going to redress your incision, and I want you to get plenty of rest. We'll be getting you up in a couple of days. That's all the goof-off time you have. Then you're going to have to start helping the recuperating process. In all seriousness, you are one lucky woman. I'll be back to check on you this evening." With that said, he left.

CHAPTER 30

AFTER THE NURSE had the dressing back on, Jeff came back and said he'd like to talk to Leslie alone.

He sat down and took Leslie's hand again. They looked at each other for a few seconds. Then Leslie said, "How's Emma? Is she really upset?"

Jeff said, "She's doing much better now. She went to the zoo with Constance and John. All she was told was that you weren't feeling well and that I was with you. I just talked to her and told her you were much better, but it would still be a while before you could come home. She said to tell you that she loves you and she'll be a good girl. Don't worry. They're taking good care of her."

"I know they are. I just don't like to be away from her this long. What day is it? The doctor was saying something about forty-eight hours. And did you get to talk to Walt?" She was stumbling over her words.

"It's Sunday afternoon. And, yes, I got ahold of Walt. He's very relieved that you woke up, and he'll be calling you in a couple of days. He wants you to rest as much as you can," said Jeff. "I'm so glad you woke up, too. I agree with Walt. You need to get plenty of rest."

The nurse came back in and gave Leslie a drink of water and then sponged off her face and arms, carefully. That seemed to relax Leslie enough so that she could go back to sleep.

Before she did, she said to Jeff, "You look tired. Will you take a nap, too?"

"I think that's a good idea. May I still hold your hand?"

As she held it out to him, she closed her eyes. Jeff said his thanks to God and closed his eyes, too, for a well-deserved sleep.

CHAPTER 31

LESLIE'S NAP LASTED until 7:30 the next morning. When she awoke, Jeff had already taken a shower and shaved and was on his second cup of coffee.

Leslie asked the nurse, "When can I start getting up? I know that the sooner I do that, I will be able to go home. I have to get back to Emma."

The nurse started to argue with her, but Jeff intervened. "You might as well call the doctor and check with him. You know her and how stubborn she can be."

"Yes, I do," said the nurse. "I'll call him right now. Just remember, Ms. Garrett, when you talk him into letting you go home, I go with you."

As she went to call the doctor, Jeff said to Leslie, "You've met your match."

After the doctor, reluctantly, gave his ok, Jeff and the nurse, carefully, got Leslie to a sitting position on the edge of the bed. Leslie was in more pain than she cared to admit, and she was feeling a little nauseous. But she didn't say anything. As they got her to her feet, she wobbled a little, but wouldn't let them stop. They finally got her to the chair, and she sank into it, gratefully. Jeff covered her with a blanket, while the nurse changed the bed. Then she got some soap and a pan of warm water to give Leslie a better sponge bath. Jeff, of course, went into the other room to make more phone calls. The nurse changed Leslie's dressing, gave her the bath and put her in a clean gown. When this was done, Jeff came back and they got Leslie into bed.

CHAPTER 32

"JEFF, I THINK you need to go home now," said Leslie.

"Are you sure? I can stay as long as you need me," he answered.

"I do need you. I need you to assure Emma that I'm all right. Don't get me wrong. I couldn't have gotten this far without you being here. But, it's time to take care of yourself, too. I also think that you're the only one who can make sure Emma is good. Please, do one more thing for me," Leslie pleaded.

Albert came to pick up Jeff and his extra things. When Albert came over to Leslie to kiss her cheek, she noticed that he had tears in his eyes.

"It's so good to see you. We miss you at home. We've all been taking real good care of Emma. She misses you, but she's ok," said Albert.

"Thanks, Albert. I miss all of you, too. I appreciate all that's been done for Emma. Tell her I'm getting much better and will be home soon." Leslie was trying her best to keep things under control. She didn't want to break down now.

Jeff came over to say his good-bye to her. "Are you sure this is what you want?" he said.

"Yes, it is."

"Ok. I'll call you tonight to see how you're doing."

After Jeff left, the room seemed to lose some of its energy. But, Leslie refused to let that take her down. She wanted to get out of here as soon as possible.

CHAPTER 33

THE DAYS WENT along with a routine. She was again pushing herself as hard as she could. Jeff and his family would call and visit. She wouldn't let them bring Emma, though. She didn't want Emma to see her until she came home. But she did finally talk to Emma on the phone. Emma was happy to talk to her mother, but Leslie was crying after the call ended.

That weekend, Leslie got a surprise visit from Walt. He came in with her favorite red carnations in his hand. "Hey, I thought I'd see a sick person in here. You look terrific!" he said, only half-joking.

"Walt, I thought you were still on location," said Leslie, very pleased to see him.

"I wasn't satisfied with phone calls. I told them that I had to have the weekend off to come and see for myself that you were ok." He walked over and gave her a kiss. The nurse took the flowers and went off to look for a vase, using that to give them some privacy.

"I'm so glad to see you," Leslie said. "And the flowers smell wonderful. How long can you stay?"

"Not long, I'm afraid. I have to leave early tomorrow morning. I guess I was lucky to get this much time. I think they thought I would explode if they didn't give into me and let me have these two days off," he said with a chuckle. He pulled up the chair that Jeff had used, took her hand and said, seriously, "How are you, Leslie? Tell me the truth. I've been so worried about you. I'm sorry I couldn't get here until now."

So Leslie told him everything that had happened. By the time she was through, Walt had turned slightly gray and had tears in his eyes. To her, it just seemed like she was talking about someone else. She still couldn't quite accept what Franklin had done to her.

Walt and Leslie talked all afternoon, with Walt telling her about the movie he was making and all the oddball things that were going on with the cast and crew. When Jeff called that evening, Leslie told him about Walt being there so they only talked briefly. Shortly after midnight, Walt said, "I have to go. I need to check on some things at the house and get back to the airport to catch my early flight. I'm glad I came here to see you. It was really hard to be there and not know what was happening here with you. Now I can rest easier since I can see that you're getting better."

"I'm glad you got to be here, too. It seems like forever since I have seen you. When you get home for good, I'll be home and recovering there. I don't plan on being here much longer," said Leslie.

"Well, don't bully the doctor too much," Walt said laughing.

"I won't. I'm just going to work hard. I need to get home."

Walt got up and kissed her good-bye. "I'll call you as often as I can, and I'll see you soon."

After Walt left, Leslie went right to sleep. It was wonderful having him with her, but she still got tired easily. Tomorrow was going to be another day of rehabilitation and she needed to be rested.

CHAPTER 34

L ESLIE HAD BEEN in the hospital for two weeks and had finally talked the doctor into releasing her after lunch. Her injuries were healing well enough and she had promised him that she wouldn't do anything taxing. He would come out once a week to check on her and make sure she was behaving herself.

Jeff and Albert came to pick her up. She was so happy to be going home she couldn't stand it. Going without seeing Emma for two weeks was as bad to her as the 'incident'. After all, Emma was her life.

Albert and Jeff gathered her things while Leslie got into the wheelchair that she was required to take out to the car. She was so anxious to go home that she was afraid she'd get to the door of the car and the doctor would stop her from getting in and make her go back inside the hospital. Boy, talk about paranoia. But, in the long run, she was helped carefully into the car and they took off for home.

CHAPTER 35

WHEN LESLIE WALKED into the house (she refused to let Jeff carry her in), everyone, even Mrs. O'Brien, was standing under a sign that read 'Welcome Home Leslie'. Emma ran up to her but stopped short of throwing her arms around her mother's legs. Jeff picked her up so that she could hug Leslie. "Are you all better now, Mommy?" asked Emma.

"I'm good enough to be home, honey, but I have to get a lot of rest. And I can't do a lot," said Leslie. "But I'm happy to be home with all of you. I know I'm going to get better faster. Thank you all for everything you've done. Since it seems like Emma's grown a foot since I've been gone, you've taken good care of her."

Jeff kept holding Emma as everyone came up to Leslie. They were hugging her gently and wishing her well and telling her how glad they were to have her home. Mrs. O'Brien came up to her, put her hands on her hips and said, "You're too skinny. You haven't had enough to eat. I'm going to the kitchen now to make you a pot of tea and fix you something to eat. And eat it, you will." As she turned to do just that, she turned back around, and said with tears in her eyes, "By the way, I'm glad to have you home." She then turned back around and went on to the kitchen.

When the employees went back to their jobs, Joe and Mary came up to her and hugged and kissed her, too. Leslie said that she was tired and that she'd better go to her room to rest (and wait on her tea and food).

Emma said, "I'll go get the elevator for you, Mommy." She ran off to get it for Leslie.

Mary said, "You call us if there's anything we can do for you. Things are certainly going to be a lot happier around here now that you are home. We're all so glad that things went as well as they did."

"Yes, we are," agreed Joe. "Other than being a little pale, you look pretty good. But, I have to agree with Mrs. O'Brien. You do look a touch thinner than before."

So Jeff and Emma went up with Leslie and got her settled in her easy chair. Emma put an afghan over Leslie to make sure she was warm enough. By that time, Julia came up to get Emma. "Why don't you get your swim suit on, and we'll go out to the pool, Emma."

"Ok, Julia. Bye, Mommy. I'll see you later. I love you," Emma said as she gave Leslie a kiss.

"I love you, too."

As Emma and Julia left the room, Anna Marie got there with Leslie's tea and a blueberry scone. Leslie realized that she was hungry after all. So when the tray was set on her lap, she took a sip of tea and a bite of scone and sighed with relief at the normalcy of things now that she was home.

Jeff sat on the sofa and chatted with Leslie while she ate. When she was done, he noticed that Leslie's eyes were drooping. So he took the tray, suggested she take a nap and told her to let him know when she was awake. By the time he was out the door with the tray, Leslie had fallen asleep.

CHAPTER 36

L ESLIE KEPT TO her word with Dr. Johnson. She rested a lot and didn't do anything too vigorous. Walt came home from location in a few weeks, and he would come over to the house as often as possible to be with Leslie. They would go on short walks, and Walt would play with Emma so they could all be together.

One night at dinner when Walt wasn't there, Jeff decided to break the news to everybody about Gwendolyn. During a lull in the conversation, he cleared his throat and said, "I have an announcement to make." With Leslie and his parents looking at him, expectedly, he said, "I've broken off my engagement to Gwendolyn."

No one knew what to say. Secretly they were all glad about this news, but they didn't want to say so. They finally all spoke at once giving their condolences. Jeff started laughing at them saying, "Seems to me, I'm the only one who's happy about this. Don't worry. I'm fine with it. It took me a while but I finally realized that I was never in love with her. We're both better off this way. That's all there is to it. So don't feel sorry for me. And we don't need to talk about it again."

After a few seconds, they all went back to eating their dinner and chatting away.

Since Jeff had told about his broken engagement, he decided to start dating again. He had his choice of women to go out with. They were never in short supply. He would go out with them for a few times and then go on to someone else. The tabloids listed him as the city's most eligible bachelor.

One day Mary said to Joe, "I'm glad Gwendolyn is out of the picture, but I'm not sure I like the way Jeff is compensating for her absence."

"I don't think you have anything to worry about," Joe replied. "He's just getting used to the fact that he's free to do what he wants. He'll tire of this and slow down. Mark my words."

CHAPTER 37

B Y THE TIME the hiatus was over, Leslie had recovered from her injuries. She was still seeing Walt. Joe and Mary were still waiting for Jeff to come to his senses about his dating habits.

On the first day back to work, people were coming up to Leslie and telling her how glad they were that she was ok and was able to come back. She had told Jeff on the way to the studio that she was nervous about being there, but felt better after all the attention she was getting.

Jeff had already made sure that security measures had been strengthened and that all the dressing trailers were kept locked. This reassured her, too.

And so the new season started. Ratings were going well and the writers were doing a fantastic job. Jeff was more involved than ever with the show. He and Leslie still ran lines on the way to and from work, but Jeff seemed to be more distant from her and everyone else, too. When he was home, he stayed in his room. When he ate dinner with the family, he rarely spoke unless spoken to.

Emma asked Leslie, "Mommy, what's the matter with Sir? He doesn't act right and he hardly ever talks to anybody."

Leslie answered her, saying, "I don't know, honey. He's been working hard. Maybe he's just tired." But, somehow she didn't think that was the problem.

One day at work, Leslie was bringing Jeff his coffee and overheard Jeff speaking to one of the crew. No, it wasn't speaking. His voice was raised and he told the poor kid, "That's your job and I expect it to be done by Monday. If you don't know how to do it, find somebody to explain it to you."

After the kid left, he turned to Leslie and grabbed the coffee out of her hand. Taking a sip, he started yelling at her, "If I had wanted a cold cup of coffee, I'd have asked for one. If you can't bring me a hot cup, get someone else to start getting my coffee." At that, he stomped off to his dressing room. Leslie just stood there staring after him. She usually had a mild temperament, but she was doing a slow burn. She took the coffee back and left the studio.

Leslie saw Albert waiting on them and she stopped to tell him that she would be taking a cab home. When Jeff came out to the car, Albert gave him the message. Jeff didn't say a word and raised the glass between them.

When Leslie got home that evening, she went directly to her room and changed clothes. She then went to the kitchen and told Mrs. O'Brien she wouldn't be home for dinner. Then she told Julia she was going for a walk and would Julia watch Emma for her.

CHAPTER 38

L ESLIE WENT OUT the gate and started off at a brisk pace. She was mad and scared at the same time. She was mad at the way Jeff had talked to a crew member and at her. She was scared because maybe Jeff was getting tired of having her and Emma there and that he might ask them to leave. As much as she had NOT wanted to live there in the first place, she had grown into loving to be there. They had all become her family. She just kept walking and walking. It got dark, but Leslie didn't notice that. All at once it started raining. It didn't happen very often that that area had a heavy rain, but it figured that since she was a good distance from home, that they would get one now. Leslie was getting soaked. She realized she was close enough to Walt's home that she could go there.

Charles opened the door and he saw Leslie standing there looking like a drowned rat. He hurried her in the house and called for Walt.

When Walt saw Leslie, he stifled a laugh because she looked so pathetic. He told Charles, "Charles, can you go turn on the shower in the guest room and take care of Leslie's clothes?"

"Yes, Mr. Walt. I'll also make a pot of hot tea and some snacks." Off he went to take care of the shower. Walt led Leslie up the stairs and took her to the guest room.

The hot water felt so good to Leslie. She had been starting to shiver from the cold of the rain. While in the shower, she started to cry. The release of the tears felt good, too. After she got out of the shower, she dried off with soft, thick, warm towels. She had given her clothes to Charles so she put on the terry cloth robe that was hanging on the door. There were warm fuzzy slippers, too.

CHAPTER 39

GOING DOWNSTAIRS SHE found Walt in the living room, where he had started a fire. It really felt good to her. She was still upset about everything that had happened, and the fire was comforting. Charles had made good on his promise to make hot tea. Sitting on the couch, Walt poured her a cup and told her to eat some of the food that was on the tray.

After Leslie had taken a sip of tea, Walt said, "Ok, now tell Uncle Walt what's going on with you. Why were you out there in the rain?"

Taking a deep breath, Leslie said, "I was taking a walk when it started raining, and I was closer to here than home."

"I think there's more to it than that. You looked upset when you got here, and you still look upset. Tell me the truth."

Deciding that Walt wasn't going to let her explanation go, she said, "Jeff has been in a bad mood for some time now, and today things came to a head. He yelled at one of the crew and then me. He's never been this way, and I think he wants Emma and me to leave."

"Has he asked you to?"

"No, but I don't understand why he's acting this way," said Leslie.

Walt put his arm around Leslie's shoulders and said, "I think you need to just put this out of your mind for now and relax." He leaned over to kiss her. "I think I know what the real problem is."

"You do? What is it?" asked Leslie, curiously.

"I want you to think about this before you say anything. I think you're in love with Jeff." As she started to deny this, he put his finger to her lips. "I said, think about it first."

Leslie was quiet for a while. Suddenly, Walt saw tears begin to well up in her eyes. "I never thought I would love anybody again. How can you know something like that about me when I never knew it myself?"

Walt smiled and said, "Leslie, I love you, and you've always been honest with me about your feelings. I've thought it for a while now, but tonight you've just shown it. The reason you didn't know it is because you don't want it to be true. You still feel like you need to be true to your husband. But he's dead and you have to finally get that through your head. Do you honestly think that he'd want you to live the rest of your life being a martyr to him? What if it was the other way around and you were dead? You'd want him to go on with his life and find someone else to love."

By this time, Leslie was openly crying. Walt gave her his handkerchief, and she wiped her eyes and blew her nose. "Walt, I love you, too. As a great friend. I feel like I've been hit over the head. I just don't know what to say. I guess I DO love him, but I'm confused about his attitude toward me now. I'm certainly not going to tell him. And this needs to be kept between us. If he has changed his attitude about me, I'm not going to go begging him for his love."

"You know I won't say anything. I'm asking you to be positive and see how things play out. Can you do that?"

"I guess I have to."

"Leslie, I'll always be there for you, no matter what. You have my shoulder to cry on. Now, I want you to finish your tea and eat some more. If you don't, Charles will blame me."

So to keep Walt out of trouble with Charles, Leslie drank her tea and ate some more. They stopped talking and just enjoyed the fire. Before too long, they had both fallen asleep.

CHAPTER 40

SOMETHING WOKE LESLIE. It took her a few seconds to realize where she was. Looking at her watch, she saw that it was three o'clock in the morning. By this time, Walt had awakened, too.

"Walt, it's late. I need to get home," Leslie said anxiously.

"Leslie, just go upstairs to the guest room and I'll take you home in the morning," said Walt, sleepily.

"No, I have to go home now. People will be worried if I'm not home when they get up. They don't even know where I am."

"Ok, I'll take you home. Charles left your clothes over on the table. Go get dressed and we'll get going."

Leslie let herself into the house and quietly went up the stairs. She checked on Emma and then went to her room. She closed her bedroom door, turned on the lights and started to go to the bathroom. She jumped when she saw Jeff sitting on her couch with a drink in his hand and a bottle of whiskey that was almost empty.

"Jeff, you scared me. What are you doing here?"

Slurring his words, he said, "I'm waiting on you. Where have you been? It's late."

"I don't think that's any of your business where I've been. Besides that, you're drunk. If you want to talk, let's make it tomorrow when you've sobered up." Leslie was getting angry.

Finishing his drink in one gulp, Jeff put his glass down and got up from the couch. Coming over to her, he backed her up against the wall and put his hands beside her shoulders. Leaning in to her he said in a voice that was deathly quiet, "Where.. have.. you.. been?"

He was so close to her that she could smell the whiskey on his breath. She should have been scared, but somehow she wasn't. "I was at Walter's."

She could see not only the anger, but the pain in his eyes. "Did you sleep with him?" When she didn't answer him, he shouted at her, "You slept with him, didn't you?"

Pushing his arms away, she moved away from him. "No, I didn't sleep with him. And even if I did, why do you care? You've been cold to me for weeks and today you yelled at me over cold coffee."

Jeff leaned his head against the wall where Leslie had just been and said, "Because I love you." He said it so low that Leslie wasn't sure she had heard him right.

"What did you say?" she whispered to him.

"I said, because I love you." With that, he walked out of the room and went to his bedroom.

CHAPTER 41

A FTER TOSSING AND turning, Leslie finally got up at eight thirty and got dressed. She was trying to decide what to do when there was a knock on the door. "Come in," she said.

When the door opened, there was Jeff with a tray with coffee and croissants. Sheepishly he said, "May I come in?"

"Of course, it's your house," Leslie said sarcastically.

"Ouch, I deserved that. Can we talk? I'm sober now."

Leslie indicated to him to set the tray down and sit on the couch. "I think that's a good idea. You go first."

Jeff poured their coffee and tried to decide how to start the conversation. "First, I owe you an apology. I'm sorry for last night and for yelling at you yesterday. I have been acting like a jerk for a few weeks." He stopped and drank some coffee.

"If you're waiting for an argument from me on that, you'll be waiting for a while. Why have you been acting like a jerk?"

"When the 'incident' happened, I was feeling pretty guilty about it. But when I thought you were going to die, I realized how I felt about you. That's when I knew I loved you and couldn't live without you."

"Why didn't you tell me then?"

"I didn't want to scare you off. You had been through a lot. You still seemed to be attached to your husband. So I thought I would wait for a while until you were better. But then you started seeing Walt even more than before. When you ran off so suddenly yesterday, I was afraid that you would take Emma and move." This all came out of his mouth in a rush of words. "When you didn't come home right away, I did the only thing I could think of – getting drunk."

Leslie sat there looking at him for a few seconds until she burst out laughing. Jeff looked at her with shock until she stopped. "I'm sorry for laughing, but you don't know the significance of that statement. You see, I thought that you wanted Emma and me to leave. That's why I went out. When the rain started, I went to Walt's. I took a hot shower, drank tea, and fell asleep in front of the fire. When I woke up, I got dressed in my clothes that Charles had cleaned for me, and Walt brought me home. Jeff, I'm not in love with Walt. And we've never been to bed."

"You're not? You didn't? I really feel like a fool now." But Leslie didn't miss the relieved smile on his face.

"I haven't been to bed with him because I love you."

Now it was Jeff's turn to start laughing. "How long have you known this? Why didn't you tell me?"

"I didn't realize it until last night when Walt told me."

"Walt had to tell you that you were in love with me? How did he know?"

"He sensed it. And even if I would have known it sooner, I wouldn't have come to you first. I was hanging on to the thought that I would be cheating on my husband if I was in love with someone else. But Troy wouldn't want that. Walt made me look at a lot of things that I had been ignoring. I have decided to quit hiding my feelings, not only from you, but from myself."

"Then I would like to ask you out to dinner tonight. You know, a date."

"I'd like that."

Getting up from the couch and pulling Leslie to her feet, Jeff kissed her with passion. "I had to do that, but I'm not going to rush you into anything. I can wait until we get married."

"Are you proposing?" Leslie asked breathlessly.

"No. You'll know when I do."

CHAPTER 42

THE DATING WENT on for several weeks. Joe and Mary were ecstatic about this new development. Jeff and Leslie were so much happier. It showed in everything they did and said. To Leslie's delight, Jeff even apologized to the kid on the crew who he had been nasty to. It didn't take long for the news to get around that they were now a couple. The tabloids said how the bachelor king was dead. He had a woman now who fit him. Women all over the city who had had their eyes on him were crushed.

Finally Jeff decided he needed to pop the question. But the setting had to be the perfect one. He elicited his parents for help.

"Mom, I need you to help me with Leslie. I need you to get her out of the house on Saturday for several hours. I also want her to have a spiffy new dress, shoes, and all the trimmings. I know it's a tall order, but if anybody can do it, you can," said Jeff.

"You know I'll be willing to do anything to help you. Your father and I are so happy about the two of you being together. This is so exciting! What do you need from me?" asked Mary.

Jeff explained his idea for proposing to Leslie.

"Jeff, you know your mom and I will do anything we can to make this plan a success," said Joe. "We think it's a great idea. Leslie will love it – and she deserves it, too."

As Jeff made the calls on Friday that he needed to do to carry off his "PTLD" (propose to Leslie day) plan, Mary was approaching Leslie with her part. "Leslie, dear, I need your help."

"Of course, Mary. What do you want me to do?" asked Leslie, eagerly. As much as Mary had done for her, it felt good to be able to reciprocate.

"Joe and I have this unexpected dinner to go to tomorrow night, and I need a new dress, shoes, the works. Can you go with me tomorrow and help me pick them out?"

"Of course, I can."

Step one done.

Saturday started step two of "PTLD". Mary and Leslie left the house to go shopping. Mary needed to keep Leslie from getting home before six o'clock.

They went to a lot of stores. Mary "couldn't find a thing" that she liked. She also made Leslie try on outfits, too. They even stopped for lunch, which Mary managed to turn into a longer-than-usual affair. It finally got late enough that Mary decided that the next store had better have the right outfit for both of them.

The gods were with them. The next store had two beautiful dresses with matching shoes and accessories. As Leslie was checking herself in the mirror, Mary "got a call" from Joe. He told her that she needed to come right home because they had to leave earlier than he thought. Leslie protested when Mary told her they had to leave.

"Mary, I can't just walk out of the store in their clothes."

"Oh, don't worry about it." Mary led the way out of the store, throwing over her shoulder to the sales girl to "put it on my account."

Step two done.

While Mary and Leslie were shopping, Jeff was finishing up his part of the plan. When he was sure that everything was perfect, he took his shower and got dressed in his tuxedo.

CHAPTER 43

MARY HAD TIMED things so good that they arrived home at almost exactly six o'clock. She stopped at the front door to let Leslie out. Then she went to put the car in the garage. At least that's what she told Leslie. She actually went to pick up Joe so they could get out of the house. They were going to Candace's house (where Emma already was) to spend the evening. The house was empty as Jeff had given everyone the night off. Of course, they all knew about "PTLD".

When Leslie went to open the front door, it opened before she had a chance to. Opening it was Edward, the owner of one of Jeff and Leslie's favorite restaurants.

Before Leslie had a chance to say anything, Edward said, "Good evening, Ms. Garrett. Would you follow me, please?" He turned and started walking toward the elevator. Since Leslie didn't think asking questions would do her any good, she just followed him.

When they got to the third floor, Edward led her to the hallway balcony door. He opened it and let Leslie go through the door first. When she turned the corner, a brilliant sight greeted her eyes. There were small white lights everywhere. A round table, in the corner was set elegantly for two people. There were colorful carnations everywhere and soft music was playing in the background. Jeff was standing in front of her with a beautiful corsage of white carnations in his hand. Leslie was so overwhelmed that all she could do was stand there looking around, taking it all in.

Jeff walked over to her, pinned the corsage on her, and leaned over to give her a kiss on the cheek. "May I have this dance, Ms. Garrett?"

asked Jeff, softly. Not waiting for an answer, he took her in his arms and started dancing to the music.

"Leslie, are you ok?"

Coming out of the shock of this beautiful scene, Leslie said, "I guess I'm so surprised, I don't know what to say."

"Do you like it?"

"It's the most beautiful thing I have ever seen. Did you do this for me?"

"Yes, I did. I had help, of course," he said, grinning like an ornery little boy with a secret.

"So, I gather your mother didn't need a new dress?" asked Leslie, beginning to catch on to how things were evolving.

"No, but I wanted you to have one. I had to get you out of the house so I could set this up. By the way, you look beautiful."

"Your mother has good taste," she said.

"I believe it runs in the family."

At that point, Edward announced that dinner was served.

Jeff led her to the table and pulled out her chair for her. When dinner was served, she noticed that Jeff had ordered all her favorites. While he ate steak, she had a lobster tail. They both had baked potatoes and asparagus. For dessert, there was crème brulee. Everything was done to perfection. After dinner, her favorite champagne was served.

She told him, "I have probably gained ten pounds this evening, but it was worth it. Thank you."

"Well, how about another dance to work off some of those pounds?"

While Edward cleared the table, they danced some more. They couldn't take their eyes off each other. When Edward was finished, he quietly left. They never even noticed. When that song was over, Jeff led her over to the cushioned bench that went all the way around the balcony. As Leslie sat down and adjusted the skirt of her dress, Jeff pulled a small box out of his pocket and got down on one knee. Leslie gasped and put her hands over her mouth as Jeff said, "Leslie Elizabeth Garrett, you are the most beautiful woman I have ever met. I remember the first time I met you. Somehow I knew that you were going to be a very important person in my life. I love you with all my heart, and I can't imagine spending the rest of my life without you in it. Will you do me the honor of becoming my wife?"

"Oh, Jeff. Yes, I will," she said as tears flowed down her cheeks. For once, they were happy tears.

Jeff took out the ring and put it on her finger. It had a colorful round opal in the center with four smaller opals down each side of the band.

Leslie asked, "How did you know I loved opals? And where did you find such a beautiful ring?" She kept turning her hand so that she could see the ring from all angles.

"I know it's your birthstone so I had it made just for you."

"Thank you so much. For everything. I don't think I have ever felt so loved and appreciated in all my life. I think I'm the honored one to get you for a husband."

Jeff got up, sat beside her, and kissed her until it took her breath away. "I want to show you that even though I'm a California man, I don't want you just for what you can give me. This relationship means a lot to me, and I want our first love making to be very special. So, even though I would like nothing better than to pick you up, take you to bed, and ravish you, I am going to wait until our wedding night."

"You ARE a gentleman, Jeff," said Leslie.

Step three done. PTLD complete.

CHAPTER 44

AFTER AN AMAZING evening, both Leslie and Jeff slept surprisingly well. The next day when they came down to breakfast, everyone was in the dining room waiting on them. Mrs. O'Brien had outdone herself, and there was enough food to feed an army. They announced their engagement, and Leslie showed off her ring. Jeff went to Emma and asked if she knew what they were talking about. She stopped eating her toast long enough to calmly look at Jeff and say, "Yes. It means you're going to be my new daddy." To her it just seemed very simple. Of course, things aren't usually complicated to children. To Emma, it was no big deal.

Jeff called for attention. He said, "By marrying Leslie, my ultimate goal was to become a father to this lovely young lady." Everyone laughed just as he had intended. "Since Leslie got a ring as a present, I thought it only appropriate that Emma should get a present." Now he had Emma's attention. Jeff pulled another little box out of his pocket, got down on one knee before Emma and asked, "Emma Elizabeth Garrett, will you do me the honor of becoming my daughter?"

Giggling, Emma, throwing her arms around Jeff, said, "Oh Daddy, you're silly. Of course, I will." Opening the box, he took out a delicate necklace with an amethyst hanging from the chain. "Daddy, it's so pretty. And it's my birthstone. Thank you very much. I love you."

Leslie thought to herself, "This is why I love him. I will never have to worry about his relationship with Emma."

Emma was going around and showing everyone the necklace her new daddy gave her. Leslie went over to Jeff and asked him how he got to be such a sensitive man. He told her to thank his parents.

CHAPTER 45

WORD SPREAD QUICKLY about the engagement. The couple started receiving cards and letters of congratulations from friends and fans. To Leslie, it was overwhelming. They even got one from Walt who had a P. S. for Leslie: "I told you so." What a sweetheart. Leslie blushed at this and Jeff just had a big grin on his face.

Life went on in the Harrington home. Jeff told Leslie that he wanted her to have the wedding of her dreams. He knew that her first wedding was a few minutes at city hall. But Leslie had other things on her mind.

One day when they were together watching a movie, Jeff noticed that Leslie was off in her own little world. So he asked her, "Hey, Ohio, are you here with me or dreaming about the wedding?"

"Neither. I need to talk to you about something that's been bothering me. It's rather personal."

Suddenly, Jeff felt nervous. "You aren't having second thoughts about marrying me, are you?"

"No, but after we talk, maybe you might." Taking a deep breath, she just spilled it to him. "You know I loved Troy with all my heart. But the feelings I'm having for you are making me feel that the love life I had with him wasn't the best that ours could be. Troy and I were high school sweethearts and married right out of school. He loved me, but I think the only thing he knew about making love was what he learned from his friends. It was ok but there was nothing magical about it. I'm afraid that I'm going to disappoint you." By this time, Leslie was blushing. She was a shy person and had been alone for so long that this was a hard subject for her. But she needed to be honest with him. The worst thing would be to get married and have him regret his decision.

Jeff took his time in answering her concerns. Finally, he said, "First of all, I am disappointed. Not over WHAT you told me, but the fact that you could think that I'm so superficial as to base a marriage only on sex." Then, taking her hands in his, and with a gentler voice, he said, "Leslie, I love YOU. If we never were able to make love, I would still love you and want to be married to you. I don't need to tell you that sex is a very personal thing. We'll figure it out together. I don't want you thinking that what you had before was the only way. You were kids and we're adults. Please forget about that time. It will be wonderful between us. I want you to just concentrate on the wedding. The rest will work itself out. Ok? Can you trust me about this?"

Breathlessly, Leslie said, "Yes, I can. I guess I just needed to hear it." Relieved, she snuggled up to him and, actually, started seeing the movie.

After that conversation, Leslie felt lighter than ever. She and Jeff were happy, and the whole family shared in that happiness. They would take Emma to the zoo and to the park for family picnics. Life was good.

CHAPTER 46

WHILE JEFF AND Leslie were still working and their days were as busy as ever, Leslie was still trying to figure out the kind of wedding she wanted. She knew she wanted more than she had the last time, but she didn't want the huge one that Jeff wanted her to have. He told her money was no object and to spend as much as she wanted. But she wasn't comfortable with that. Besides, this was important to her, and she didn't want a lot of people there who didn't really mean anything to her.

One day she came up with the perfect solution for her. It was a compromise to both options. She figured that if Jeff could surprise her when he proposed, that she could do the same thing with their wedding. And, as Jeff had done, she engaged the help of Joe and Mary.

Leslie managed to get them alone together in their bedroom. She was excited to enlist their help in her scheme. She had only been in their room once before, but she remembered the elegant, yet cozy surroundings. She loved the ivory and gold brocade wallpaper and the beautiful Louis XVI chairs and sofa by the fireplace.

"I want to thank both of you for helping me out with this project. I love Jeff, but he wants too big of a wedding for me. If I told him about this idea of mine, he would think that I'm only doing a small affair because I don't want to spend the money it would take for a bigger affair."

Joe said, "Leslie, I agree with that. He thinks the bigger the better. Sometimes that's ok, but you should have what you want. Besides, turnabout is fair play. I think this is going to be wonderful. Let's get started."

"I'd like to have the wedding here. Outside by the pool. Would that be all right?" Leslie asked hesitantly.

Joe, right away said, "Of course. That would be a beautiful place to have it."

"Thank you."

"Mary, will you, Constance, and Candace help me pick out a wedding dress for me and a flower girl's dress for Emma?" asked Leslie.

"We'd be delighted. Oh, Leslie, this is going to be so much fun. I can hardly wait. What date are we shooting for?" asked Mary.

"I know this is short notice, but I'd like to have it the Saturday before Thanksgiving. That's in three weeks."

"Well, we've got our work cut out for us. We'll need to check on flowers, music, catering, and guest list. Let's get started," said Mary.

"One last thing," said Leslie. "Joe, will you give me away?"

"I would be honored," said Joe, beaming.

CHAPTER 47

T HE DAY OF the wedding was here in the blink of an eye. To be able to set up without Jeff knowing about it, Joe had arranged for Jeff and him to play golf. He planned on playing thirty-six holes. They left at eight a.m., and the wedding was scheduled for four-thirty. As soon as the men were gone, people came in rapidly to get things set up. Since all the employees were to be guests today, they were not allowed to do anything. The only exception was Julia, who was in charge of getting Emma ready. Mary and Leslie were there to make sure that everything was set up the way Leslie wanted it.

There was a stage covering the pool. This is where the ceremony would take place. The florists came and put up flowers everywhere. All the female guests were to have white carnation corsages, and the men were to have white carnation boutonnieres. Jeff was to have a red boutonniere, and Leslie would be carrying a beautiful red bouquet. While most women wanted roses, Leslie had always loved the look and aroma of carnations. Even Emma was to throw carnation petals from her basket. Leslie didn't want them to have attendants except Emma.

The band was to set up at noon for music at the reception, and there was to be a string quartet for the ceremony.

Leslie had already set up the menu for the dinner. Appetizers were to be available as soon as the ceremony was over. This would give the caterers time to set up the tables outside. There was also to be an open bar, which included champagne. The cake was a combination of Jeff and Leslie's favorites. She was a white cake fanatic, and he loved chocolate. The tiers were alternated and all was covered with a delicious buttercream frosting. The cake was decorated with frosting carnations.

Leslie had spared no expense on all of these things. Yet the cost was still probably a quarter of what Jeff would have wanted her to spend.

With things well under control, everyone went to their rooms to get ready for the big event. Leslie took a leisurely, scented bath. She then got dressed in lacy undergarments and a robe. The women were there to do her hair, nails, and makeup. While that was being done, Mary came in to be with Leslie. Even though Mrs. O'Brien wasn't supposed to work that day, she insisted on sending up to Leslie a pot of her favorite tea and some cookies. She told Leslie that "unless you want to faint during the ceremony, you'd better eat and drink everything." Knowing Mrs. O'Brien would be disappointed if she didn't partake in the refreshments, Leslie did as she was told.

After the ladies had finished with Mary and Leslie, they left to do Emma's hair. There was time enough for Mary and Leslie to relax and talk before Leslie had to get dressed. She was so pleased with the dress she had found. She couldn't believe the luck she had in finding it. It was of the palest blue – so pale it almost looked silver. It had a low bodice and back with cap sleeves. Her favorite part was the flow of the gown and the chapel train. When she first put it on she twirled around, and the gown billowed out around her. It was the most beautiful thing she had ever seen. She knew that Jeff was going to love it on her. Her veil was chapel length, too, and attached to her hair at the back.

She had found a perfect white dress that was appropriate for Emma. Emma wanted a veil too, so a little one was made for her. She looked adorable.

CHAPTER 48

JOE AND JEFF had a great day on the links. They both played well, and the weather was just right. It wasn't too hot or too cool. After they played, they went into the clubhouse to have lunch. While they were eating, Jeff asked his dad what he was doing the rest of the day.

Joe said, "I'm going to a wedding."

"Oh. Who's getting married?" Jeff hadn't heard about this before.

Without missing a beat, Joe said, "Yours."

Jeff choked on his drink and looked at his dad dumbfounded. "What did you say?"

Joe couldn't help but laugh as he said, "I said yours. Do you think you're the only one who can plan a surprise?"

"But, Dad, a wedding is a lot bigger than the proposal night I planned." Jeff was still in shock over the news.

"The difference, Son, is that there were women planning this. You will soon learn what they can do when they put their minds together."

"Ok. Now I want to hear the details."

"Jeff, Leslie knew that you wanted her to have the wedding of her dreams. It's just that your idea and her idea of a dream wedding were very far apart. Don't get me wrong. It's going to be beautiful. And she's getting everything she wants. She didn't scrimp on money, but she didn't spend money just to be spending it," said Joe, proudly.

"What time IS this wedding?" asked Jeff. He was starting to get used to the idea – and getting excited.

"The festivities begin at four-thirty."

"Well, Dad, let's get going. I've got to get ready for the biggest day of my life."

CHAPTER 49

WHEN JOE AND Jeff got home, they went straight to Jeff's bedroom. Joe had strict orders to keep Jeff from seeing any of the wedding decorations until it was time for the ceremony.

Joe said, "Your tux and everything else you need is hanging in your closet. I'll come back to get you around four-fifteen. I need to go get in my fancy duds. Your mother will probably have some other things for me to do, too. These women have been rushing around planning this for three weeks now. From what I've seen, they've done a great job. Mary seems ten years younger. She's had so much fun. Your sisters have done their fair share, too. Most of the time us men have just stayed out of the way."

Jeff had gone to his desk and gotten two small boxes out and handed them to his dad. "I've had these waiting for a while now. They're marked on top. One is for Leslie and one is for Emma. Will you deliver them for me, please?"

"Of course. I'll do it right now." Hesitating a few seconds, Joe went to his son and gave him a hug. "Jeff, I hope you know how much this wedding pleases your mother and me. I think we both would have been heartbroken if the two of you weren't getting married. We love you both – and Emma, too." That having been said, he turned, got out his handkerchief and wiped his eyes and blew his nose. Then he left to do his errands.

Jeff went to his desk and again got out another small box. It had the wedding rings that were to be Leslie's. They had been made at the same time her engagement ring was made. There were two rings – one for either side of the engagement ring. On top, they had a horse-shoe effect, so they circled the large opal with smaller opals. They, too, each had four opals down the sides of the rings. Saying that the set was breath-taking was rather an understatement.

Then he went to take another shower and get dressed.

CHAPTER 50

WHEN JOE DELIVERED the box to Leslie, she had put on her gown and veil, and the photographer and videographer were busy with pictures. When Leslie opened the box, the photographer caught the expression on her face perfectly. She took out a necklace that matched her rings. It was a round opal centered inside a lacy heart with chips of opals surrounding it. There was a note from Jeff: My darling soon-to-be wife. A woman has to have a necklace to match her wedding rings. So I had this made especially for you. I had the opals put inside the heart because that's where I hold you – deep within my heart.

"Joe, will you put this on me, please? Isn't it beautiful?"

Everyone oohed and aahed over it. Leslie vowed she wasn't going to cry, because she didn't want to ruin her makeup. But it was difficult. Just then Julia and Emma came in the room. Leslie showed them the necklace, which they both loved.

Joe said, "Emma, I have something for you from Jeff." He handed her the box with her name on it. She tore off the paper and opened it. Inside was a bracelet to match the necklace he had already given her. Her note read: To my new daughter-to-be, Emma. I had this made special for you. I love you so very much and am so proud to be your new father.

At exactly four-fifteen, Joe walked into Jeff's room and told him it was time to go. When they got downstairs, Joe took Jeff around and showed him everything that had been done for the wedding. The guests were seated, and the quartet was playing softly. Jeff said hello to his guests, and then Joe led him to where he would stand next to the minister.

"Here is where I leave you, Son. You'll be fine."

"Thanks, Dad, for everything."

CHAPTER 51

STEPPING OUT OF the elevator, Mary went first to take her seat. The music was still playing softly. Julia took Emma to the doorway and reminded her of what she had to do. Then Julia took her seat beside Anna Marie. Emma did exactly what she was supposed to do. When she got to where the ceremony was to take place, she went to Jeff. He leaned down and gave her a kiss. She showed him that she had his necklace and bracelet on and whispered, "Thank you" to him. Then she went to sit with Mary.

When Leslie and Joe got to the doorway, the quartet started playing the Wedding March. As Joe and Leslie walked toward Jeff, he choked up with emotion. She looked amazingly beautiful. It suddenly struck him that this was exactly the perfect wedding for them. If it was any bigger, it would have been just a public display of wealth. As it was now, it was intimate and meaningful.

Coming out of his reverie, he saw that she was beside him, smiling at him with adoration.

The ceremony went rather quickly. Since the wedding was a surprise to Jeff, Leslie had decided to use the traditional wedding vows. When they turned to walk back down the aisle, Emma ran over to them so that she could be with them. Jeff picked her up with one arm while he held Leslie's hand. They were now a real family.

While the formal pictures were being taken and the tables were set up, the guests were indulging in the wonderful appetizers that the caterers had made.

When everyone went to sit down, dinner was brought out to them. The menu was simple: chicken and steak, baked potatoes, and asparagus. Simple and delicious. During dinner there were plenty of toasts, including one from Walter, who took claim to getting Leslie and Jeff together. Everyone laughed because they didn't know what part he had played in their relationship.

When the cake was brought out, Leslie and Jeff cut a slice as was tradition. Jeff was impressed that it was both chocolate and white.

While cake was being served, the band had started to play dance music. Jeff and Leslie danced the first one. Then they both danced with Emma. After that, everyone started to dance. By this time, Emma was starting to yawn. Julia said she would get Emma to bed. "No," said Emma. "I want my Daddy to put me to bed." Julia said, "Why don't we go on up and get your jammies on and Mommy and Daddy will both come up and tuck you in."

"Ok," said Emma.

Julia went over and told Leslie and Jeff her plan. They agreed and said they would be up in ten minutes.

When they got upstairs, Emma was in bed, still yawning. She said, "I already said my prayers and I prayed for Mommy, my old Daddy, my new Daddy, my new Grandma and Grandpa, my new Aunts and Uncles, and cousins."

Jeff said to her, "Wow. That was a mouthful, honey. Now it's time for you to go to sleep. Did you have a good time today?"

"Yes, Daddy. Can we do it again?" Leslie and Jeff both groaned.

"I think we'll have to wait a while for that," said Leslie. "Now good night, little one."

Jeff said, "Don't let the bedbugs bite."

CHAPTER 52

WHEN THEY GOT back to the reception, Jeff and Leslie found everyone dancing and having a very good time. The appetizers were back out for people to snack on and there was still cake, champagne, and other drinks. Jeff and Leslie joined in the fun. It truly was a great party. Finally, about four a.m. the party broke up. Everyone declared that it was a party no one would ever forget.

Jeff and Leslie went up to Jeff's (which was now Leslie's, too) bedroom. In anticipation of the time when Leslie would be in there, Jeff had done some remodeling. What had been his bathroom and closet had been torn out and enough added on to make a bathroom and closet for each of them. The bathrooms were side-by-side with their closets on each side of the bathrooms. It was a woman's dream set up.

The rest of the bedroom suite was still the same. The room was done in shades of blue and had a fireplace and TV in both the bedroom section and the sitting room area. The woodwork and bedroom furniture were the same as Leslie's old room. The living room furniture was overstuffed and very comfortable. Jeff had brought Leslie's easy chair from her room into their room.

They both went into their bathrooms; Leslie to take a fragrant, soothing bath and Jeff to take a shower. When he was done, Jeff came out in silk pajamas and robe. He sat down to wait for Leslie and poured himself a drink. He had started a fire and was reading when Leslie came out in a very simple white satin nightgown.

As he looked up at her, Jeff was again amazed at her beauty. He got up, went to her, and kissed her with the passion that had been building since the ceremony. She returned that passion to him. She was shaking slightly. Jeff wasn't sure if she was cold or scared. For her, it was anticipation.

He asked her, "Are you ok with this? I don't want you to be afraid. I love you so very much and, no matter what, we'll be ok."

Leslie said, "I'm all right. I'm not scared. I trust you completely."

"You wanted me to teach you how to make love and I will. But, if there is something you don't like or want me to do, just say so. I will always respect your wishes. We have to make a promise to each other. If either of us isn't in the mood, that person has to say so. And there will be no hurt feelings on either side. Promise?"

"I promise. We have to base everything in our life together on communication," said Leslie.

With that promise, Jeff took off his robe, then slid the thin straps off Leslie's shoulders and let her gown slip to the floor. He then picked her up and gently placed her on the bed. He took off his own pajamas and got into bed beside her. He again kissed her and then began touching her. She reacted to his touch in a positive manner, so he continued. All the while, he whispered, lovingly, to her. He ran his finger down between her breasts and then her stomach until he felt her scar that was left from the 'incident.' He continued to caress her body until he felt her shudder and moan his name. Only when he knew she was satisfied did he satisfy himself. When he was done, he lay beside her and ran his finger up and down her arm while planting little kisses all over her neck and face.

Catching her breath, Leslie asked, "Was I ok for you?"

"Well, maybe a little better than ok." He was teasing her and she started giggling. Then, nuzzling her neck, he whispered, "Seriously, sweetheart, you had nothing to worry about. You were amazing! If you keep this up, you're going to wear me out."

They lay there side by side and talked about their future and what they wanted out of life for each other. It wasn't long before they both fell asleep. They had been up for almost twenty-four hours, and it had been an exciting day and night.

Leslie woke up first and lay there watching her new husband and thinking about her previous one. She loved them both and yet they were very different from each other. But one was in the past, and she must put all her heart into the present. She started to run her hand over him as he had done to her. He woke up quickly at the pleasantness of her new passion, and they made love again. After that, they decided that if they were to continue down this path, they needed nourishment. Jeff called down to the kitchen and asked If someone could bring them a hearty breakfast (even though it was almost noon).

They each took a quick shower and by the time they were dressed, breakfast was there. After a meal of eggs, bacon, croissants, fruit, tea and coffee, they were sated (with food, that is).

CHAPTER 53

AFTER BREAKFAST, THEY went downstairs and found Emma and her grandparents outside. Emma and Joe were playing in the pool while Mary was reading a magazine. Everything had been cleaned up from the previous day's festivities. Jeff and Leslie sat down with Mary and had some iced tea with her.

Emma saw them and got out of the pool to run to them for hugs and kisses. Then she ran back to the pool and jumped in so she could splash Grandpa Joe. He pretended to be angry, and then splashed her back. They both laughed and continued to play.

"Are you two going to go away for a honeymoon or are you going to hang around us old folks?" asked Mary.

Jeff and Leslie looked at each other. Neither one of them had even thought about a honeymoon. So it was somewhat stunning when Mary talked about it.

"Mom, we hadn't even thought about it," said Jeff. "Honey, do you have someplace you'd like to go?"

"Well, I can't think of anywhere. I was concentrating so much on the wedding that I didn't even think about it. What are you thinking?"

"I just figured that when we decided on the wedding date that I would think about it then."

Mary said, "I have a suggestion, if you want to hear it."

They both said, "Yes."

"Why don't you go up to the cabin for a week? I can call Fran and Bart and have everything stocked for you. It will be quiet, and you can do whatever you want without a lot of people watching your every move. You both could use some rest."

"Mary, I think that's a wonderful idea. I would really like that. What do you think, Jeff?"

"I'm wondering why I didn't think of it. Would you call them and let them know we'll be up there later this evening?"

"I'll call them right now."

"We'll say goodbye to Emma and then go pack," said Jeff.

CHAPTER 54

THEY WERE ON their way. Leslie had heard about the cabin but had never been there. Jeff told her that Fran and Bart were neighbors who they hired to be caretakers for the place. The cabin was another place that his great grandfather had built. Jeff hadn't been there for a while, and he was looking forward to having time alone with Leslie for the next week.

They didn't talk very much on the drive up to the cabin. But, the silence seemed comfortable. Leslie wanted Jeff to be able to concentrate on his driving. Some of the mountain roads could be hazardous, and she didn't want to distract him.

They came to Fran and Bart's cabin first. When they stopped, the couple came out to greet them. Jeff proudly introduced Leslie to them. The ladies hit it off immediately and had all kinds of things to talk about.

"I have the cabin all cleaned up, and there's plenty of food in the pantry, fridge, and freezer. There are clean towels in the bathrooms and fresh sheets on the beds. Leslie, I know you're going to love the place. Please let me know if you need anything at all. I can get you whatever you need."

"I'm sure that you have things taken care of just fine," said Leslie. "And we didn't give you a lot of notice that we were coming."

"Bart and I were so excited to hear that Jeff had gotten married. Mary sounded so happy when she talked about you. I can see why, too. I like you and I think Jeff did pretty good for himself."

Leslie blushed at the compliment and said, "I think I'm pretty lucky, too. Jeff is going to be a great husband and a wonderful father to my, I mean our, daughter, Emma."

"Mary told me about her new granddaughter. She couldn't say enough about her and how much joy she has brought into their lives."

"She loves her so much. I don't know what I would do without her and Joe. I couldn't have gotten better people for in-laws if I'd have picked them out myself."

"You're right about that. They've always been good to us," said Fran.

The guys came up to them just then. They had been talking about various things around the cabin that Jeff might need to know.

"You should have plenty of firewood, but if you find you're running out, just let me know, and I'll bring another load up to you," said Bart. "Now, Fran, we need to let them get settled in. They probably want to get a fire started and get some dinner into their bellies. Here's the key, Jeff. We'll be here if you need anything."

Jeff and Leslie got in the car, waved goodbye, and took off up the road for the cabin. When they got there, Leslie gasped as they rounded the bend, and she got her first look at it. Their 'cabin' was a two-story, three bedroom, three-and-a-half bathroom, cabin-style house with a wrap-around porch. It was so quaint and homey. She loved it immediately.

"This is what you call a cabin?" she asked. "My old apartment would fit in here – twice."

"I guess we do underplay it. Wait until you see the inside. If we can't rest here, we can't rest anywhere. You're going to love it. My parents used to come up here five or six times a year. But not so much lately."

Jeff was right. Leslie walked in and saw the overstuffed couch and chairs. There was a huge fireplace with a thick, white, fluffy rug in front of it. The lighting was dim for effect but could be turned up so that a person could read or do activities. The kitchen was off the living room but was open so that anyone in the kitchen was still a part of whatever was going on in the living room. The kitchen was bright and cheery and had all the necessary appliances. There was a counter-top bar with four barstools for casual eating. There was also room in the living room for a larger table, if needed. There was also a half bath to one side.

When they took their bags upstairs, Jeff had Leslie look around at all the bedrooms. She found each room to have large, comfortable-looking, canopied beds, lush carpeting and an attached bathroom. Each room was done in a different soft color scheme. There was one that was gray and one that was blue. The one they picked for themselves was a beautiful soft green.

After they unpacked, they went downstairs and Jeff started a fire, while Leslie checked out the kitchen to see what they could have for dinner. She found two steaks in the fridge, potatoes for baking and broccoli. By the time Jeff had the fire going and came into the kitchen, Leslie had dinner going.

Jeff fixed them each a drink while they waited for dinner.

"I never asked if you could cook. I guess it's a good thing you can, because my cooking skills are limited to the barbecue grill," Jeff said.

"I can cook – not as good as Mrs. O'Brien, but at least we won't starve while we're here."

When dinner was ready, they ate at the bar. Then they cleaned up the kitchen together. Jeff poured them another drink, and they sat on the fluffy rug in front of the fire. Before too long, they started kissing. Jeff wasn't pushy, but he was certainly passionate. As he awakened Leslie's passion, she became more open. He made her aware of the things that her first husband had discouraged her from doing. Jeff made her feel important and unashamed to try new things. Things she had always wondered about. With Jeff, nothing was forbidden, and he encouraged her questions. Every day they were at the cabin brought them closer together. It seemed as though they had known each other forever.

For the next week, they took walks together, cooked and ate together, read, and watched movies together, and, of course, made love together. It was a dream week.

When the week was up and they had to go home, it was as if they were one person. Neither one had ever felt for another as they did for each other.

CHAPTER 55

I T WAS LATE when they left the cabin, so they just dropped the key off in Bart and Fran's mailbox and drove slowly home. When they got there, everyone was asleep. So they left the bags in the car and went up to kiss Emma. Then they went to their room. They were back in reality land now. They were both exhausted from the drive. Even though they were too tired for lovemaking, they still curled up next to each other and fell fast asleep.

The next morning, Jeff and Leslie went down to breakfast. They weren't expected so everyone was surprised to see them. Emma rushed over to them and managed to get her arms around both sets of legs.

Jeff asked, picking her up, "How's my little girl?"

"I'm fine, Daddy. Did you and Mommy have a good time? We went to Aunt Candace's house and Aunt Constance's. We went swimming and shopping, too," said Emma with excitement.

"We had a good time, but we missed you. I'm glad you had a good time. Now you need to eat your breakfast." He put her down and gave her a big smooch.

Breakfast was extra special that morning. Everyone seemed to be talking all at once and sharing their week with each other.

CHAPTER 56

LIFE AGAIN SETTLED into a regular routine. Jeff and Leslie went back to work. The first day back, they were met with applause from everyone on the set. Then the congratulations started. Leslie felt as welcome as when she returned to work after she was sick. This was much better, though.

In February, Emma turned six-years-old. She was already going to kindergarten. But turning six seemed like a big deal to Leslie. Her little girl was getting bigger.

By the end of April, Leslie felt like she was getting a touch of the flu. Normally she was a pretty healthy person, but since she had pneumonia she didn't want to take any chances on getting sick again. She decided to take more vitamins and keep an eye on things. If she got a fever or started to feel worse, she'd go see Doc.

One day at work, she had just given Jeff his morning coffee when down she went. She passed out right at his feet. It happened so suddenly that Jeff didn't have a chance of catching her. People gathered around her. Jeff handed his coffee mug to someone and picked her up to take her to his dressing trailer. He called back over his shoulder for someone to call Doc and get him out there.

Jeff put her in the bed and put a wet wash cloth on her forehead. By the time Doc got there, Leslie was awake and feeling foolish. She tried to get up, but Jeff wouldn't let her.

Doc came in and sat in the chair next to the bed. He took her temperature, blood pressure, and all those little things that doctors do.

He said to them, "Your blood pressure is elevated, but that's to be expected right now. Tell me how you've been feeling lately."

"I thought that maybe I was getting the flu, but I wasn't feeling bad enough to call you. Then all of a sudden I woke up here. I don't remember fainting or feeling dizzy or anything."

"Well, you seem fine, but I'm going to draw some blood and run a few generic tests to see if I find anything. Why don't you go home and rest until I get back to you," Doc said to Leslie. He drew blood from her arm and then left.

Jeff said, "I'm sure you're ok, but why don't you take a nap, and I'll have Albert drive in and take you home."

"I'll take the nap, but don't have Albert make a special trip in to pick me up. I always have my book with me. I can just read until you're ready to go home. I promise I'll rest."

"Ok, but I'm going to check on you as often as I can get away."

"I'll be here."

When they got home that night, he told his parents what happened that day and that Leslie was going to be staying home for a while.

The next morning when Jeff got up to go to work, Leslie tried to get up with him. But Jeff wouldn't hear of it. Despite what Doc said, he was concerned about Leslie's health. He had almost lost her once, and he didn't want to think about possibly losing her now.

CHAPTER 57

SATURDAY, DOC CALLED and said he had the results from Leslie's blood work. He dropped over to the house, and they met with him in the den.

"Doc, you sounded so serious on the phone. What's going on?" asked Jeff. "Is it bad news? Just spill it, please."

"Just calm down, both of you. It's good news. Leslie, you're pregnant." He waited until his words sank in. When they did, Jeff and Leslie hugged and kissed each other. Then they were hugging Doc.

"Ok, ok, enough. I'm just the messenger. There's more I think I should tell you. I've set up an appointment for you with the best OB doctor in Los Angeles. His name is Dr. Jenkins, and you're to see him Monday afternoon at two p.m. Can you make it?"

Jeff said, "You bet we can. They'll just have to shoot around me. Do you think anything's wrong?"

"No. I'm just anticipating what I know would be the next thing you'd ask me for." Doc then went to Leslie and said, "I'm so happy for the two of you. I'll still be there for you. Don't think you've gotten rid of me."

Smiling, Leslie hugged him. "That would be the last thing I'd want to do. He'll send you a copy of all the records, and I want you to let me know if you don't agree with him."

"That's already been arranged. Goodbye, happy people."

They found Jeff's parents in their room. Mary was reading, and Joe was watching TV. They were ecstatic when they heard the news.

"I was hoping for more grandchildren, but I didn't expect it so soon," said Joe.

Mary said, "I guess this is your 'flu', Leslie. The best kind to have. Let's all sit down and have some tea. You both look a little pale."

They all sat down, and Mary poured tea for everyone.

"Mom, we have an appointment with a Dr. Jenkins on Monday. I think we should wait until after we see him and then decide when and what to tell everybody," said Jeff.

"I've heard of him and it's been nothing but good. Does Doc think there's a problem?" asked Mary.

"No, he just knows Jeff," said Leslie. "I don't think it's a bad idea, though.

"Of course, it's a good idea. You have to take care of yourself," said Mary.

They finished their tea and Joe said, "I think we need to celebrate this special occasion – at least among ourselves. I want to take the four of us out to dinner. So, ladies, get dolled up, and I'll make reservations."

"Sounds like a plan, Dad," said Jeff.

CHAPTER 58

W HEN THEY WENT to bed that night, Jeff and Leslie snuggled together. Leslie was half asleep when Jeff said, "Les."

"Hmmm?" she asked sleepily.

"I must be the most naïve man in the world." Ok, that got her attention.

"Why do you say that?" she asked, more wide awake.

"I never even considered the fact that we could have another child. I was completely satisfied with you and Emma. You know she means everything to me."

"I know that, and I think it's sweet that you think that way. But, the fact is, we're going to have a baby. Are you upset about it?" Leslie was getting a little nervous now.

"Upset? Not in the least bit. I just don't think it's sunk in yet. I think after we see the doctor, it will seem more real. You go to sleep now. You need all the rest you can get."

Agreeing with him, Leslie snuggled down, again and was asleep within a minute.

Jeff and Leslie had gotten into the habit of being lazy on Sunday mornings. They stayed in their pajamas, drinking coffee or tea, reading the morning paper or a book. They did this in the sitting room of their bedroom suite. They were doing just this when Emma ran in with exciting news.

"Mommy, Daddy. Grandpa and Grandma are taking me camping next week, and we're going fishing, and sleeping in a tent, and everything."

Leslie said, "Are you sure that's what they said, honey?"

Jeff put down his paper and said, "I'm sure they did, Les. They used to take my sisters' kids camping, too."

"But, Jeff. That was a long time ago. Are they still up to it?"

Emma interrupted, "Mommy, I have to go get my stuff ready. We're getting ready to leave. I just came up to tell you good-bye." She then went to her parents and gave them each a hug and kiss. Then she ran out to get ready.

"Jeff?"

"Les, let's go for a walk." He grabbed her hand and took her around the third floor until they came to the back where they could see out. "Now, look out there, and tell me what you see."

"It looks like a tent."

"That's right. Albert put it up for them. That's where they 'camp' out. They use the pool house bathroom. They have a campfire going, and that's what they cook over. The folks love it, and the kids have usually been about Emma's age so they love it, too." Jeff turned to walk back to their room to finish his paper.

"But, Jeff. Didn't Emma say something about fishing?"

He stopped, turned to look at her with a smirk on his face. "What do you think the pool is for? Dad had it stocked yesterday with fish. Close your mouth, dear."

CHAPTER 59

LESLIE HAD HAD her examination with Dr. Jenkins, and both she and Jeff were sitting in his office so that he could talk to them. Since Jeff was new to this process, he was quite nervous. Even though Leslie HAD been through this before, she was still nervous.

Dr. Jenkins said to them both, "I've read your health history and your previous pregnancy history that was sent over to me. These two things plus the examination of today shows that you should have a healthy baby. I'm concerned about the fact that you did have a little trouble in your last pregnancy. I'm also concerned about the attack that was made on you. While I don't believe that either of these things will hurt the baby, between the two you might have to go on bed rest. I noticed that your morning sickness has been fairly extreme. Are you keeping food down?"

"What I eat seems to stay down, but I'm not able to eat very much in the first place," said Leslie.

"I think you should keep track of what you eat and how much. You can show me that the next time you come in. Then I can decide if you need to add anything to your diet. Instead of the usual monthly visits, I want to start out by seeing you every other week. Mr. Harriman, you've been very quiet. Do you have any questions?"

"Dr., I've just been trying to take it all in. This is my first time going through all this and, right now, I can't think of a single thing to ask you. I'm sure I'll have a lot of questions later."

"Don't feel bad. Most of the first-time fathers feel this way. Just write down the questions you come up with and fax them over to my office. I'll get back to you with the answers. Now, Mrs. Harriman, your history says that you work. Is it a necessity?"

"No. We don't need the money," said Leslie.

"Then I would advise you to quit and stay home. I want your stress level down as low as possible. I also don't want you doing a lot of hard work. No heavy lifting. Stay away from stairs as much as possible. And the worst news is, no intercourse. I know you're newlyweds, but I think you should abstain from that, too. I want you to call me if you feel like something isn't right. Day or night. My job is to help you have the healthiest baby possible. Do you have any questions?" asked Dr. Jenkins.

Leslie thought for a minute or so and said, "If I have to go on bed rest, how long would that be for?"

"It's hard to say. It could be a few weeks or it could be a few months. We'll just have to wait and see."

After leaving the doctor's office, Jeff and Leslie drove out to the 'camp site' to tell Joe and Mary about the visit. They decided to tell Emma so that she wouldn't find out by accident.

When they got home, they walked out back and found Joe and Emma 'fishing' in the pool. Leslie thought it was the silliest thing she had ever seen – but also the sweetest. The two of them were talking and having the best time together. Emma needed time with her new grandparents. How many others would go to all this trouble for a child who was no blood relation to them? Not many.

Jeff called out to them, "How's the fishing today?"

Emma called back, "I caught two fish. Grandpa caught three. We're going to have them for dinner. Grandma's going to cook them for us."

"That's wonderful, honey. We're going to go talk to Grandma now."

When they found Mary, she hugged them both and asked how things went at the doctor's.

Leslie was bringing Mary up-to-date while Jeff went to see how the fishing was coming along. They were just getting their gear together. Emma showed him their fish, and then she ran ahead to let Mary know it was time for dinner to get started. Jeff and Joe walked a little slower and Jeff told Joe about the doctor's visit.

"Dad, I want to make sure Les is taken care of and that her stress level stays down. I think that's going to be the worst thing for her and the baby. But, I'm not sure I can do that without letting her know how scared I am."

"Jeff, I understand how you must feel. It's hard enough to go through your first pregnancy. But to go into it knowing there could be a problem just makes things seem worse. Don't let her think you're too capable. Tell Leslie about your feelings. If you don't, she'll pull away from you. You can do anything as long as you pull together, Son."

"Thanks, Dad. I don't know what we would do without the two of you," said Jeff.

"Well, hopefully, you won't have to know that for a while, anyway," chuckled Joe.

Mary and Joe were cooking dinner while Jeff and Leslie talked to Emma. She was sitting on Jeff's lap.

Jeff said to Emma, "Mommy and I have a surprise for you, Emma." That got her attention. "You're going to have a little brother or sister. Mommy's going to have a baby. Won't that be exciting? You're going to be a big sister."

"I am?" she asked. "What does a big sister do?"

"Well," said Leslie. "You can help give it a bath and play with it. You can rock it and talk to it and read it stories. There's all kinds of ways to be a big sister. We're really going to need you. Can you do that?"

"Sure, Mommy." Leslie could almost hear the wheels turning in Emma's mind. Then Emma asked, "Can I have a brother?"

Jeff and Leslie smiled at each other and Jeff said, "We'll work on that and see what we can do. But, we'll just have to see."

Just then Mary announced that dinner was ready. She got Emma settled and asked Jeff and Leslie if they would like something to eat. Jeff turned to Leslie, noticed she was turning a pale shade of green and told his mom that they were just going to get some soup and put Leslie to bed.

They told Emma good-night and went into the house. While Leslie went upstairs and got into her old, comfortable sweats, Jeff went to the kitchen and found some homemade chicken soup simmering on the stove. He knew that, once again, Mrs. O'Brien had anticipated their needs. The kettle was hot, too. The teapot was ready to go, and she had also put dishes on a tray. All he had to do was pour the water into the teapot and ladle soup into the bowls.

He took the tray and went upstairs. Leslie was settled in her chair and looked much better. She was still pale, but at least she wasn't green anymore. He gave her the soup and poured her a cup of tea. She managed to eat most of the bowl of soup and drink all of her tea.

CHAPTER 60

J EFF AND LESLIE spent the next week getting acclimated to another new lifestyle. Jeff went off to work without Leslie with him. Neither one were happy about that, but had every intention of doing what the doctor told them to do. Leslie wanted to get up with him in the mornings and see him off, but Jeff wouldn't hear of it. He said she was to get as much sleep as possible. Secretly, she was relieved because she was always so tired. She still couldn't eat very much either. She did the best she could, but her stomach had the upper hand, so-to-speak.

When the week was up, the threesome came home from their camping trip. Mary said to Emma, "We had such a good time. Would you like to go camping again?"

"Yes, can we?" asked Emma.

Joe answered, "You bet we can. We'll take you to the cabin in the mountains, too, if you want."

"I'd really like that, Grandpa."

The next day, Mary took Emma to Candace's house so that Joe could take care of the pool. He had the fish that were left over taken out and the pool was drained, cleaned, and refilled. While that was going on, Albert was taking down the tent, and Julia and Anna Marie were getting bedding and miscellaneous items into the house. It was a busy day, and normally Leslie would have been glad to help, but she just wasn't feeling up to it. By this time, all the help knew that there was to be a new baby in the house. You could feel the excitement in the air.

The next time Leslie went to the doctor, Jeff couldn't go with her. They were trying to wrap things up for the season, so he couldn't leave. Mary went in his place. Dr. Jenkins didn't do an examination this time. He wanted to see how she was getting along.

He asked her if she was able to eat more, but wasn't surprised when she said no. He could tell by looking at her that she had lost weight. "I'm not feeling very good about you and food. I'm going to give you a better vitamin, and I want you to try to drink some Ensure. Let me know if you can't get that down. I think I can safely assume that you aren't getting around much because you're exhausted, right?"

"Yes, you can safely assume that," said Leslie.

"Well, keep trying to get as much nourishment as you can, and I'll see you in two weeks."

"Thank you, Dr. I'll do my best."

CHAPTER 61

L ESLIE TOLD JEFF that night what the doctor said. He wasn't
surprised. He had seen the weight loss himself. Whenever he put
his arms around her, he felt more bones than the last time.

"Jeff, I do try to eat. You know that, don't you?" she asked.

"I know you do, honey. But, I'm getting really concerned for you."

"Let's go down to dinner, and I'll try harder."

"Ok."

They went downstairs and found Joe, Mary, and Emma already at
the table. Jeff pulled out her chair for her.

Mrs. O'Brien came into the dining room and said, "I getting
frustrated with your eating habits, lately. You're just wasting away. I
haven't made anything spicy and have made all your favorite foods. I'm
running out of ideas. Tonight, I've made one of your favorite dinners.
There's turkey, stuffing, mashed potatoes and gravy, and asparagus. If
this doesn't do it, then I give up." She then went back to her kitchen,
shaking her head.

Everyone was chatting away. Leslie was doing her best to eat. She
knew how Mrs. O'Brien was trying so hard to cook for her. She wanted
to please her and everybody else, especially Jeff, by eating as much as
she could.

Emma was being very quiet tonight and not eating well, either.
Finally, she spoke up. "Mommy, what is your last name?"

Surprised at this question, the others became quiet.

Wondering where this was coming from Leslie said, "It's Harriman,
sweetie."

"And Daddy's, Grandma's, and Grandpa's last name?"

"It's Harriman."

"What will be my new brother's last name?"

"Honey, it will be Harriman. What's going on?"

"If everybody else's name is Harriman, why isn't mine?"

Jeff and Leslie looked at each other in surprise. They were wondering how long Emma had been thinking about that.

Finally, Jeff said to Emma, "Honey, you have your first daddy's last name. I guess we never thought about it, because it didn't make any difference to us. You're my little girl. I love you. So do Grandma and Grandpa and all your other family."

Emma was upset now and she said, with a raised voice, "But my name isn't Harriman. I don't belong to anybody." She got up from the table and started to run from the room. She turned and screamed at Jeff, "I'm not your little girl, and you're not my Daddy." With that she ran from the room.

Leslie got up quickly and started to go after her. So did Jeff. But the excitement was too much for Leslie and she fainted before she got two steps away from the table. Jeff got to her, lifted her up, and told someone to call Dr. Jenkins. He got her upstairs to their bed and put her down. Mary got a cool, wet washcloth to put on her head. Joe called the doctor.

Jeff said, "Mom, I've got to go to Emma. Please watch Leslie."

"Of course."

On the way to Emma's room, Jeff met Joe going to Jeff's room. Joe told him that the doctor was on his way to check on Leslie. When Jeff got to Emma's room, he found her lying face down on her bed, sobbing. He picked her up and held her to his chest and let her continue to cry while he stroked her hair and murmured soothingly to her.

She finally stopped crying and gave out a few hiccups. Jeff pulled her away from him so he could see her face. He pulled out his handkerchief and wiped the tears from her eyes. He then gave it to her to blow her nose.

When that was done, Jeff said to her, "You know I love you, don't you?"

She nodded her head, yes.

"Emma, I'm sorry you don't think I'm your Daddy. But, to me, you ARE my little girl. I love you as much as I'm going to love your new brother or sister. Your name has nothing to do with that. You must have been thinking about this for a long time."

Again, she nodded, yes.

"I wish you had talked to us before about this. Now that I know how you feel about the name and how important it is to you, it is important to your mom and me. So I have an idea how we can fix that. I haven't talked to your mother about this, but I have a feeling she'll go along with it. Do you want to hear my idea?"

"Yes."

"Ok, here it is. None of us want you to forget your first daddy. But I want you to know that you are mine. I will go to the judge and ask him if I can adopt you. I'll also ask him if your new name can be Emma Elizabeth Garrett-Harriman. What do you think about that?"

Emma thought about it for a little bit. Then she threw her arms around Jeff, hugging him tightly. "Oh, Daddy, can we please do that?"

"We sure can."

"I like it. I'm sorry I said the things I did. I was mad. I didn't mean to hurt you or Mommy."

"I know you didn't, sweetheart. From now on, I want you to promise me that if you get something on your mind that you will come to your mom and me and talk to us. No matter what it is. Ok?"

"Ok, Daddy. Can I go talk to Mommy now?"

"Why don't you stay here, and I'll have Grandma and Grandpa come and take you out for ice cream? Mommy's taking a nap right now."

"Ok, Daddy."

CHAPTER 62

THE DOCTOR GOT to the house quickly. Leslie was awake by then and was upset about Emma. Jeff told her what he had talked to Emma about. She thought his idea was a good one and calmed down a lot. It seemed like she couldn't cope with things as well as she used to. Pregnancy hormones.

After the doctor had checked her out, he walked over to the fireplace and thought about the best thing that could be done. Finally, he came back to them and said, "I think you're going to need to go on bed rest. You need to get a private-duty nurse to come stay with you during the day. You can get up to use the bathroom. You can get up once a week to take a shower, and the rest of the time, the nurse can give you sponge baths. I'm also going to get you an I.V. You need to hydrate some more. Continue to try and eat whatever you can. I know you've been trying to do what I ask, but we need to help that along. I'll check your file and call the nurse you've had before. Is there anything else I can do for you?"

Leslie said, "No. I'm actually feeling better having the decisions made for me."

"Then I'll be going so I can get the arrangements made."

Jeff leaned over and gave Leslie a kiss on the forehead and said, "I'm going to walk the doctor out, and I'll be right back. Then we can talk."

As Jeff was walking out with the doctor, he said to him, "Thanks for coming out here, Doctor. Is there anything else I can do to make things better?"

"I would tell you to make sure she does what I tell her to do, but I don't think we have a problem with that. She's really trying to do what

I ask. I think what she needs most is to not have to make any decisions on anything. And, of course, your emotional support. She needs rest – and a lot of it. Again, call if you need anything. I'll be checking in on her often. Good night, Mr. Harriman."

"Good night, Doctor."

CHAPTER 63

MRS. O'BRIEN PERSONALLY brought up a pot of Leslie's favorite tea. Leslie was sitting up in bed and took the cup Mrs. O'Brien handed her and was able to drink the whole cup. Mrs. O'Brien gave her another one and stayed until Jeff came back. Then she left with a smug look on her face.

Jeff poured a cup of tea for himself and pulled a chair up to the bed so that the two of them could talk.

"Les, are you really ok with what I told Emma?" he asked.

"Oh, yes, Jeff. I think that's the perfect solution. I felt just like you. I had no idea this was bothering her."

"Are you ok about having to stay in bed?"

"Yes, I guess I was worried about doing something to hurt the baby. If I stay in bed, there's less chance of that. I just hate the inconvenience this will be to everyone."

"You can't feel like that, Les. This household sticks together. We're all family. Nobody is going to see this as an inconvenience. It's just what needs to be done to have a healthy baby – who belongs to everyone. Just like Emma does."

"Ok. I'll do what the doctor says. Just like I have been. But I still want to have our Sunday mornings together. You can carry me over to the sitting room. Agreed?"

"You got it, babe. As long as you're not up walking around, I don't think it should hurt anything."

So they started another new routine. Leslie stayed in bed, Jeff went to work, and everyone took care of everyone else.

CHAPTER 64

LESLIE WAS BEING good about staying in bed. She never complained about it, but she was tired of it already. But she didn't want anyone else to know that. She didn't want anybody to feel sorry for her or, worse, baby her any more than they already were.

She so looked forward to Sunday mornings. That was the only time she felt normal. Nobody disturbed them, and they had the chance to talk. It was the best time. One Sunday, Leslie noticed that Jeff was intently reading a script.

She asked, "Jeff. What are you reading?"

"A script that was sent over to me. It's a movie my agent wants me to do while we're off this summer. I told him no, but he wanted me to read it anyway. So, to humor him, I am."

Leslie didn't say anything, but she could see the look in his eyes that told her that he DID want to do the movie.

The next day while Jeff was at work, Leslie had her nurse bring her the script. She read it and realized that the part was perfect for Jeff. She also knew he would give his eye teeth for this part. As far as she was concerned, he had to do it. So she picked up the phone and called his agent.

"Jonas. This is Leslie Harriman. I just read the script that was sent over. What did Jeff say about it?"

"He said there was no way he was going to leave you long enough to do a movie."

"That's what I thought," she said. "Well, don't count him out yet. He's perfect for this part, and I want him to do it. I'm going to talk him into it. You'll probably hear him protesting clear over to your office. I'll have him call you."

151

"Thanks for calling me, Leslie. I wanted to call you about it, but he threatened to go to another agent if I did. You are one lucky lady, my dear. I'll be looking forward to his call. Thanks, darlin'. I owe you."

"You're welcome, Jonas."

That night when Jeff came home, she decided to get right to the point. After he kissed her hello and sat down beside the bed, he noticed the script beside her.

"What's that doing over here?" he asked.

"I was bored, so I read it. It's ok. But I'm not sure why they sent it to you. Doesn't Jonas know you wouldn't do it? It's really not that good a script, anyway."

"Well, Les. It's not that bad. I guess he thought it would be a good fit for me. But I told him I wasn't going to go on location and leave you."

"Ok, enough fooling around with words. Jeffrey Preston Harriman, you know that part is perfect for you. You are NOT going to use me as an excuse to refuse to do it. I'm having a baby – not dying. I told Jonas today when I called HIM that you would call him and say that you were going to do it. Are you going to argue with me about it?"

Jeff said, "Just calm down. Are you sure that's what you want? It means my being gone for three months. I'm not sure I could even come home until it was finished."

"Jeff, I love you very much, and I couldn't stand the thought of you not doing this film because of me. It's just too important. Please call Jonas."

Then Jeff said the two words that all good husbands say to their wives, "Yes, dear."

So he called Jonas.

CHAPTER 65

JEFF HAD TO leave on the Monday after his show went on hiatus for the summer. He and Leslie spent Sunday morning together as they normally did. However, they were both feeling anxious about being separated. Even though Leslie was eating somewhat better, she still wasn't up to par. But, she put up a good front for Jeff. She couldn't have him change his mind at the last minute.

He got up early the next morning to catch his flight for New York. He kissed her and held her so tightly, he was afraid he'd break her bones. Then he went down to say goodbye to everyone else. Emma clung to him and said, "Daddy, I don't want you to leave. Why do you have to go?"

Jeff explained to her, "Honey, I don't want to leave, either. But, this is part of my job. I will miss you and your mother every day I'm gone. And, I'll be home as soon as I can."

"Ok. Daddy, you haven't forgotten your promise to me about my name, have you?" she asked.

"You know I haven't. It could take some time. Courts aren't very fast, Em. But I'm checking on it all the time. Now I have to go, or I'll miss my plane. I'm trusting you to help everybody take care of Mommy. Can you do that?"

"Of course, I can. I'm getting to be a big girl," she said proudly.

"Yes, you are. I'll call you as often as I can. You behave for me."

"I will, Daddy."

He went to the car, which Albert had brought up front. He looked up to his bedroom window as they drove down the driveway. He had to gulp a couple of times to keep the tears back. He wasn't stupid. He knew that Leslie had made a great sacrifice for him to do this project. And he loved her more than life itself.

The nurse told Leslie when Jeff's car went through the gate. Leslie knew she was going to cry, but didn't dare do so until she was sure he was gone. When he was, she burst out in tears. Enough bravery for today. She had been holding it in for way too long. When she finally got all the tears out – for now – the nurse handed her a cup of tea. Then she got a cool, wet washcloth to wipe Leslie's face so that she would feel a little better.

Just then Emma came running into the room with tears running down her face. "Mommy, Mommy. Daddy's gone. I want him to come home."

Holding her daughter, Leslie said, "It's ok, baby. Daddy will be back before you know it. Now don't cry. Daddy wouldn't want you to be sad. That would just make him sad. Here, let me wipe your face. That's better. Now you go down and find Grandma and Grandpa. I'm sure Daddy will be calling soon."

"Ok, Mommy. I'll be brave."

"That's a good girl."

CHAPTER 66

AND JEFF DID call. He called every night when he got back to his hotel. He didn't always get to talk to Emma, but he always talked to Leslie. It didn't matter what time it was because if he woke her, she just went back to sleep.

The doctor kept coming and told Leslie he was proud that she hadn't lost any more weight. She was able to drink the Ensure and to eat a little more than she had been. That was the best she could do. She was still restless, but she had a lot of company from the family and Walt, too, to keep her entertained.

One night, Jeff had just gotten back to his hotel room, when someone knocked on the door. He answered it and before he could stop her, his co-star swept in. She was a beautiful woman, and it didn't take long for him to realize that she was used to getting anything she wanted. She had made it very clear that she wanted Jeffrey Harriman but, he had managed to avoid her for a month. He had been told that she thought she would certainly be successful in seducing him.

"Jeffrey, darling. I need a drink, and I thought we could have one together," she purred.

"Certainly, Doris. Scotch on the rocks?"

"That would be fine."

He poured them each a drink, and they downed them quickly. As he went to refill his, she made her move. Coming up to him, she put her arms around him and gave him a passionate kiss on the lips.

He downed his second drink and asked, "Doris, what's the hurry? Can you wait just a minute?"

"Of course, Jeffrey."

Jeff picked up his phone and dialed. After the second ring, Leslie picked up. He said, "Honey, I'm sorry to wake you, but I just got back, and I had the funniest story to tell you. My co-star, Doris is here. She thinks she's going to get me into bed. Sweetheart, stop laughing. I know that, and you know that, but I don't think she knows that. I'm going to show her to the door, and I'll call you back."

Hanging up the phone, he turned and saw a red-faced Doris downing another drink. He said to her, "Doris, did I ever tell you why I broke off my engagement to my first fiancée? It's because she called me Jeffrey."

After Doris slammed out the door, Jeff picked up the phone again and called Leslie back. "Well, I don't think she'll try that again. To say she was mad is an understatement. I'm sure she feels humiliated, but if I hadn't have done what I did, she would have tried again. I couldn't stand that a second time. Geez, she's nobody I would want even if I didn't have you."

"Jeff, I'm glad you called – both times. I haven't been worried about you cheating on me, but there's always that very small chance that I could be wrong. I'm glad I wasn't."

"So am I. I love you. I'll talk to you tomorrow."

"I love you, too."

CHAPTER 67

FINALLY, THE MOVIE was finished, and Jeff returned home. The doctor had given Leslie permission to be downstairs for a little while. They had planned a small welcome home party for Jeff. Emma was so excited that she couldn't stand still. Finally, he and Albert walked through the door. Albert told him that he was to go into the dining room. Everyone was there. Mrs. O'Brien had cooked her heart out, and there was a big Welcome Home banner hanging over the windows.

He picked up Emma as she grabbed him around the legs, and gave her a big hug and kiss. Then he noticed Leslie sitting at the dining room table. He gave Emma to Julia and went to kneel down beside Leslie. He took her in his arms and hugged her gently. When he left, she had the smallest of baby bumps, but now she had a basketball. She returned his hug and told him to go talk to everyone else while she had a cup of tea. He did as she wanted, but kept looking at her.

When they all sat down to eat, he sat beside her and noticed that she actually ate. He leaned over and whispered to her how proud he was of her.

After the party was over, Jeff carried her upstairs and laid her on the bed. She was sitting up and he sat up beside her and took her hand. "Have I told you how much I love you and missed you?"

"Only every night. It kept me going, you know. The doctor says that he thinks I should be able to get up soon. I hope so. I still won't be able to do a lot, but just being able to get up when I want will be so nice."

"Yes, it will. I just can't tell you how proud I am of you. Not many women would be able to do this and never complain. I'm not sure how you do it."

"I do it because of you and Emma and the baby. I won't deny that it gets frustrating at times. But I just think that it must be for you and all the others, too. And I count to ten a lot. I must admit that it helped when you called me the night Doris stopped in. Every time I thought of it, I burst out laughing. That made things a lot better for me."

"I'm glad. Are you getting sleepy? I am. Let's go to bed. We can even sleep in tomorrow."

"Yes, good idea."

CHAPTER 68

TIME WAS FLYING by now. Jeff started back to work on his TV show, Emma was in school, and Leslie was allowed to get up. She still had to be careful, but had gotten a small reprieve. They were settling in, and her due date was getting closer all the time. Mary, Candace, and Constance had gone to the attic and gotten down boxes of baby clothes. They were all cleaned and separated between boy and girl.

Jeff and Leslie had decided to turn her old room into a nursery for the new baby. Julia was going to divide her time between Emma and the baby. Since Emma was in school all day now, she didn't need as much help as the new one would.

Jeff and Leslie picked out colors for the nursery. Since they didn't know the sex of the baby, and the room was already painted mauve, they just added touches of blue. The baby furniture that had been used for most of the Harriman children was also brought down from the attic. It was of a beautiful cherry wood, and Leslie loved it. The women brought up the clean baby clothes and arranged them so that they could keep one set and box up the other.

Now the only thing that was left was the waiting.

Thanksgiving came and went. Leslie was several days past her due date and feeling very uncomfortable. She tossed and turned at night because of it. She felt so bad for Jeff. She knew he couldn't be sleeping well either. But, he refused to sleep anywhere else. He had told her that he had slept alone enough when he was shooting the movie. Even with her tossing and turning, he was getting more sleep than he had then.

Then one night when she got up to go to the bathroom, her water broke. She had been having mild contractions all day, but hadn't thought anything of it. Now she realized they were the real thing. She decided to take her shower and get ready before she woke Jeff up. She knew how keyed up he was, and she wanted the peace and quiet of getting ready and taking her time doing it.

When she was ready, she woke him up. He jumped up when he realized what was going on. She told him there was plenty of time. First he called Albert to get the car. Then he took his shower and got dressed. They picked up her bag, stopped to wake his parents and by that time, Albert had brought the car around.

The next morning, Joe and Mary brought Emma to the hospital. Leslie was sitting up in bed with Jeff by her side and the baby in her arms. Emma was standing back until Jeff said, "Emma, come up here with us and meet your new little brother." Then she ran and climbed up on the bed with them. She held out her finger to him, and he grabbed it. "See, he knows you're his big sister."

"What's his name, Mommy?"

"His name is Luke Preston Harriman."

"Hello, Baby Luke. I'm your sister Emma. I brought my favorite book along to read to you."

Taking an envelope from the table, Jeff handed it to Emma. "Here's another present for you, Em."

Opening the envelope, she looked at it and read, "Emma..Elizabeth.. Garrett-Harriman. Daddy, you did it! Oh, now I belong!"

As Emma opened the book and started to read, Joe turned to Mary and said, "I think they all belong – to each other."

EPILOGUE

WAKING FROM HER reverie, Leslie felt a slight chill in her eighty-two-year-old bones. She was on the balcony, waiting on her children, Emma and Luke, their spouses, children, and grandchildren to come up the drive.

Most of the people she had been daydreaming about were gone now. Jeff's parents, Joe and Mary, his sisters, Candace and Constance, and their husbands, Mrs. O'Brien, Albert and Amy, and Doc. They had even lost Walt last year. Tearing up, she realized what a wonderful life she had had with them and, of course, her loving husband and best friend, Jeff.

There they were now. They all honked their horns at her and waved as they saw her looking down at them. She waved back. Turning she said, "Jeff, darling, they're here."

"I was just bringing you out a sweater. It's getting a bit chilly out here," said her eighty-seven-year-old husband.

Looking at him, she felt the same thrill that she had always felt when she saw him or even thought about him. He was a part of her just as she was a part of him.

Putting the sweater around her shoulders, he drew her close to him and kissed her with as much passion as he had the first time he kissed her.

"Come on, my love. They're all waiting to celebrate our anniversary. It's been fifty-five years, but it only seems like a few. I love you so very much," he said as lovingly as ever.

"I love you, too," she replied.

Hand in hand, they went down to celebrate their life together with their beloved family.

The End

Printed in the United States
By Bookmasters